H₂O

The Beginning of the End?

Karthik Vepuri

Copyright

Copyright © 2020 by Karthik Vepuri, BECOLORLESS LLC.

Published by BECOLORLESS LLC.

ISBN: 978-1-953969-05-7

Publisher's Note

Portions of this book are works of fiction. Any references to historical events, real people, or real places are used fictitiously. Other names, characters, places, and events are products of the author's imagination, and any resemblances to actual events or places or persons, living or dead, is entirely coincidental.

About H2O

Like they said in the ancient scriptures the earth starts to flood. Scientists race to determine the cause. Before they can find anything, they learn that they are running out of time. The floods keep asking questions about human existence. For once people cooperate. They are not going to give up on this battle without a fight. They come up with different solutions. Governments are helpless. They need to survive and fight this battle on their own.

Katy a teenager in her early teens thinks she can help with the situation. She might still be a child but along with her friends, they learn to celebrate human ingenuity. As they go through this journey, they discover themselves and the importance of the community around them. They fight together for human survival. With the clock ticking quickly, is this the beginning of the end? Will humans survive?

About the Author

Karthik Vepuri is an engineer who has a love for creative writing. Even though he is not a professional writer he has a passion to share his thoughts through his stories. He wants to share his ideas on the importance of cooperation and self-reliance within the communities through this story. He believes that with human ingenuity, we can dream big and achieve incredible feats that would even surprise us.

Note:

Most of this story takes place in the New York area. For the sake of the story, I have altered certain aspects and taken a few liberties with the location. The basic premise of this book is to celebrate human ingenuity and to rekindle the excitement about human possibilities. So, some of the technology mentioned in this book is a work of fiction to show the reader that it's ok to dream big. Thank you in advance for understanding the author's creative license.

Other Publications:

Children's book called "be Colorless" a story about a colorless car called Water that teaches kids about compassion, kindness, and empathy.

Cover Design:

Front cover: Photographed in Oceanside, California by Karthik Vepuri. Cover design by Karthik Vepuri.

*To my mom Madhavi, who departed this world far too
soon but left it kinder than she found it.*

Contents

Chapter One 1

Chapter Two 11

Chapter Three...21

Chapter Four 33

Chapter Five 44

Chapter Six 56

Chapter Seven 67

Chapter Eight...80

Chapter Nine 89

Chapter Ten...100

Chapter Eleven 109

Chapter Twelve 118

Chapter Thirteen 127

Chapter Fourteen 138

Chapter Fifteen 148

Chapter One

No one saw it coming. Everyone had thought it was a joke until it became as serious as a heart attack. As a young girl, my mom had told me an ancient story about how water had swallowed the earth and everything on it. Each time she read that story to me, I'd think about it all night imagining what it would be like to be trapped and buried deep beneath the grip of water. I'd think of the water entering my ears, my eyes, my nose down to my throat and filling up my lungs like a balloon, and then how my tummy would keep swelling until it just burst open. Whenever I blinked back to reality, I'd scream out of fear, hold my mom tightly, and whisper into her ears.

"Mom would the earth ever be underwater again?" my tiny voice resounding in her ears.

"No baby, the rainbow you see is up there to prevent the earth from being flooded again."

Well, mom convinced my innocent mind back then that the earth would never be flooded again but that did not stop other regions of the world from being covered with water. Water was on a mission. It wanted to poke its head again like it did in the days of the ancient story that my mom told me. It wanted to make us realize that it still had power over us. Water had a visit to earth and its first stop was my very own state, New York.

I had heard about global warming in my geography class. Mr. Stanford, the grumpy old geography teacher had taken us through the rigors of global warming and all it entails. I remember scribbling in my notes the meaning of global warming while Mr. Stanford dictated slowly:

"Global warming is a gradual increase in the overall temperature of the earth's atmosphere generally attributed to the greenhouse effect caused by increased levels of carbon dioxide, CFCs, and other pollutants." He continued.

It is an aspect of climate change, referring to the long-term use of the planet's temperature...

"Excuse me, Mr. Stanford, what causes global warming?"

I remembered there were murmurings in the class when the red-haired boy stood up to ask the question as Mr. Stanford already spelled it out in the notes. Notwithstanding, Mr. Stanford grudgingly replied as he touched the rim of his glasses.

"Global warming is caused by increased concentrations of greenhouse gases in the atmosphere, ranging from activities in the atmosphere arising from human activities such as burning fossils, fuels, deforestation, and farming."

I remember going home that day to read up more about global warming and the damage its long-term effects could cause to the earth's crust. I looked up pictures on the internet and saw cities and towns that had been flooded and destroyed. Some reporters say the ice in the polar region was melting and hence, resulting in uncontrolled flooding in towns close to the coasts. I saw children crying everywhere, as they couldn't find their parents. That night, I lay awake in bed, wondering and hoping that I wouldn't have to experience the whole flooding menace. Then I heard dad's voice roar down the hallway, and it got me running down the stairs. I couldn't believe what I was seeing. CNN had it as its headlines that Brooklyn and Bronx had experienced a massive flood that couldn't be accounted for. Those were cities around New York! I was thunderstruck. I twitched at my eyes to know if I was reading the news correctly. The water was already knocking around the doorstep of New York. My fears were being confirmed gradually. People had lost their lives to the water and thousands were homeless.

"Reports say that the sea levels are beginning to rise. Some scientists say it's due to global warming, other geologists say it might be as a result of geothermal events. Will the waters continue to rise beyond what we can handle? Will the earth be destroyed with water? ..."

I didn't wait to hear the news correspondent go on and on with the rhetorical questions. I ran back to my room upstairs and slipped under the covers. I lay there wondering what the day held in store for me, having begun that Saturday morning with an alarming news headline.

With the yawn of every sunrise, there was a simultaneous flow of water into towns and cities of the world without any warning. I was constantly glued to the news being the curious teenager that I was. I wanted to know where the next hit would be and probably call up loved ones and friends living in those areas. I wanted to hear their voices one more time just in case that would be the last. As it stood, no one was certain which city or town would be the next victim of the flood. My best friend, Tracy was living in Connecticut and they had just been hit with the flood. I was glad she was safe when I heard her voice on the phone, but I could hear the fear in her soft soprano voice.

"Katy, the flood ain't no joke. We couldn't get anything out of our house. This is fucking crazy, Katy. I'm scared. I don't think all this would end anytime soon."

I agreed with what Tracy said. All of this was insane. Having water all around you and there's not a damn thing you can do about it. Worst still, it was a natural disaster which means it's next to impossible for us to put a brake on it. We can only predict and make speculations. That was exactly what the scientists were grappling with. A group of scientists had come out to say it is solely a result of global warming and the CFCs. Another group held on to the thesis that it is a result of geothermal energy in the earth's crust. So, the arguments kept on while the water kept on its wild adventure. The last thing I heard in the news before going to bed was that the water level will rise above 50-80 feet from what it currently was, in the next decade. But what if the water rose to about 100 feet in the next year? After all, we haven't been great at predicting the weather as such. What if this was the beginning of the end? I dozed off to sleep with hundreds of questions ringing in my head.

In the months that followed, New York, located in the Mid-Atlantic region, the 27th largest US State by area with diverse geography had already become a pool of water. New Jersey and Pennsylvania in the South and Connecticut and Massachusetts in the Eastern part of New York weren't left out either. Regions throughout the US had gone into a state of global and environmental emergency along with several other parts of the world. Panic stuck when the water rose above the feet of the Statue of Liberty. Everyone knew that the world was in for some serious business and that the water ain't a joke. Lives and properties were being lost, little towns were in danger and cities were getting overpopulated by the minute. People were trooping into the main cities as the floods hadn't gotten to those areas. News correspondents and weather forecasts had predicted the next flood to hit Guttenberg or North Bergen. That was where our house was situated. Schools were shut down. Markets were closed except for small grocery stores that could be easily accessed. I kept myself busy, surfing the net trying to seek ways to curb this menace. I made up my mind that I wouldn't fold my hands and watch these floods destroy us all. I just didn't know how I was going to help out, but I knew I need to do something.

One evening after taking a walk down the street with my dog, Kula, I came home and overheard dad reading from the New York Times. Just when I was about to sit and listen, mom called out to me.

"Katy, go and wash your hands first. It's almost time for dinner."

I turned deaf ears to mom and reopened my ears to what dad had to say about the news. Finally, the government had decided that states and cities that had not been attacked by the flood, start building concrete walls to prevent the water from coming through. Brilliant! I screamed as I went to wash off for dinner. There was a solution springing forth to tackle the water. That was the first time I slept sound like a baby, not having to worry about the situation all around, as a solution was lurking by the corner.

Construction work started as soon as the day broke. The Commissioner of Environmental and Global Development had announced on the news that time was not on our side, but we could make time for our friends by doing what we had to do. I agreed with what she said, and I was willing to work as a volunteer in the building project. Every hand was on the deck. Other neighboring cities had also adopted the task of building concrete walls just to protect themselves from a common enemy, water. But the floods came without announcing their arrival on the west side of New York and the concrete was too weak to withstand the torrent of the water. Again, another city had been hit and even though they had a concrete wall around it couldn't stop the angry waves. Lives and properties took a bow again as they were being carried in the waves. Work had stopped in our region, as it was obvious that we were not making any headway. My nightmares returned, this time, much worse than the previous ones. I had seen myself being choked to death with the water filling up my insides. At once, I woke up gasping for breath. Then I knew it was closer than I imagined.

A young researcher had come up with a discovery. He had termed it the "human fish tank thesis." While he was interviewed, he explained that he experimented by being caged in a glass-cubed bathtub that he had constructed, while he left the shower running and he survived without being flooded or suffocated. When fellow researchers asked how humans were going to survive in an enclosed glass space, the young man had explained that the glasshouse would be constructed in such a way that it would be 100 feet well above sea level and the roofing would be in such a way that air would be allowed into the huge, glassed house for cross ventilation.

"That's a brilliant idea, dad! Awesome. I think this is going to work this time daddy."

I skipped around the house with Kula wagging her tail to my rhythm. I was excited, I knew that the young man's plan was going to work. The concrete wall had failed yeah, but I had a hunch that the glass cubed house wasn't going to fail.

"We would all just be human goldfishes living in a large glass tank," Dad responded and we both smiled.

Dad always knew I had a love for geography and the ecosystem as a whole. He knew that I was going to turn out to be a geographer that will provide solutions to the world's global environmental crisis. He just had that faith in me. Mom on the other hand wanted me to be a medical doctor. But she saw the passion I put into my geography classes, weather news, and high school environmental research. She accepted the fact that her only daughter was going to be an environmental geographer.

Some of the largest companies in the US came up with technology that can build glasshouses on-site. It was similar to 3D printer technology. They can build them fast and efficiently. It didn't take long for the huge glasshouse to be constructed. It turned out to be a bulletproof glass house, that was the best part for me. The US government had glasshouses constructed in major coastal cities and States to accommodate the large population. In no time, we all had moved into the giant glasshouse. It didn't have windows hanging at its side. It only had one large opening as a roof that seemed to be kissing the very clouds. Even the floor was made of glass too. It had different compartments that served as little rooms to house families that were not more than a total of eight. Large families were given another compartment. There was also a compartment for groceries and drinks. Fast food joints were also set up in some places.

There was a guiding rule that stated that each family tied a particular pattern of fabric around their right wrists for easy identification, anyone could get lost with the massive crowd around. There were toilets and baths attached to each compartment and that made me cringe. The fact that I had to share toilets with strange people sent shivers down my spine. But we didn't have a choice. We all had to survive one way or the other no matter how tough it looked.

It was large enough to accommodate well over 500,000 people at a time. Lesser populated towns were relocated to the bigger cities to avoid being swept away by the next flood, especially those situated in the danger zone and flood-prone areas. The glasshouse made me feel like I was trapped in a fish tank, but the only difference was I wasn't a fish and of course, there was no water to swim in.

"This is fucking cool. Woah!" I recognized the voice to be that of the red-haired boy that stood up to ask a question in Mr. Stanford's class.

"Hey, Katy!" he yelled.

"You know my name? But we never even said a word to each other In class."

"Yeah, I know. But it doesn't take long to discover one of the smart kids in Mr. Stanford's class. Anyways, I'm Dannie but some people call me Big Dannie" he stretched his arms out to me.

"Dannie is fine by me. Pleased to meet you, Dannie."

That was the beginning of my friendship with the red-haired dude that wore curiosity as a second skin. Families were asked to stay close to each other in the glasshouse to avoid missing a child or a relative. But children would always be children. You'd always find one mom running after her toddler to keep her in place or you'd see a young man trying to keep his son from breaking off his grip to play with other children. Kula was kept in the pet compartment with other dogs. With time I knew she was going to get used to the place just the way I was getting used to staying in a glasshouse.

It didn't take long for me to connect with my fellow high school mates. I had my cell phone with me and after dialing the numbers of two of my best friends, Andrew and Cassy, we all agreed to meet in front of the pet compartment. By the time I got there, we all hugged and recounted tales of the difficulty we all had in locating the pet shop amidst the population. With a spring in our feet, all four of us set out on an adventure to explore this glasshouse of ours. Our first discovery was that our glasshouses were being designed with the movement mechanism. You could move your hands on the glass walls and see rhythmic movements on the surface. It was fun! We spent hours that day making circular motions on the glass walls. I am glad they gave us some form of entertainment.

Chapter Two

My nightmares returned. I thought since we had found perfect safety. I had found peace, but the nightmares still haunted me. I began to wake up at night sweating profusely. I was restless. It was almost as if I knew what the heart of water felt like. I could always hear a nagging voice in my head. My problem was I couldn't risk looking crazy to my friends and family, I stayed mute. In my nightmares I found myself spending hours intrigued by water as she called unto me. Some days using my hand to trace patterns on the glass I felt water moved with the motions of my finger. Strangely I heard my name one night. I thought it was my buddies, so I skipped out of my room to go see what was up. I found an empty hallway, I thought they'd be playing a game. I followed the bouts of light leading me to the top of the glasshouse. I was about to turn around just then I heard it clearly, *"Katy you can only ignore me for so long".* I froze and with everything within me. I saw it clearly, a face: colorless, pure, and enchanting as water. It stretched and curved a form like an arm beckoning me to come. I answered with no fear at all, then I woke up.

The next time when I was hanging out with Andrew, Dannie, and Cassy, I had a lot to say to them about my endless nightmares.

"It just keeps coming guys. It's like I'm under some sort of spell to always see water ever since this whole flood stuff came up."

"Maybe it's because you love geography and the ecosystem too much," Andrew replied in between laughter.

"I guess it's probably because you've read a whole lot about natural disasters. But whatever happens Katy, there has got to be a way to end this!" Cassy firmly replied, adjusting her round-framed glasses. Cassy had lost her grandmom to the floods. She had made up her mind to put an end to this flood or at least help out with floods no matter how insignificant her inputs were. She couldn't bear risking her close relatives anymore.

We met a few of our classmates and discussions about what was happening around seemed to hang over our heads for most of the time.

The news headlines weren't getting any better. Many towns had been reduced to ruins and places with lower population were being relocated to larger ones. Glass houses were getting populated by the minute! Our glasshouse wasn't spared. We had different people trooping in. Even the homeless people from the streets and those in the poorer hoods had to be helped too. But they had their own compartment. I caught the glimpse of a young girl, barely old enough to hold a doll. Her flowery dress was stained with grease and her feet looked like they hadn't been in shoes for a very long time. Her hazel eyes seemed to have seen a lot of things that her mouth couldn't voice. She was wandering around the glasshouse turning her small head sideways now and then. She seemed lost. Yet, no one seemed to notice the poor girl or see through her glassy eyes. She had two fingers stuck in her mouth. I could tell she was very hungry.

"Hey, little girl. how are you?"

There was no response. She just lowered her head to the ground, nodding several times, her blonde hair following the rhythm of her head in return.

I tried once more to get her attention, but she just wouldn't look up. I guess she was too shy to look at me. Thankfully, I had candy in my pocket. I reached for it and squatted in front of the little girl. Just in case my height was making her scared. With the knees on the ground, I offered the candy to her and there was a spark in her eyes. Just like her eyeballs had sunlight in them. She collected the candy from my hand and a small smile lit her lips. She didn't utter a thank you. She just kept on looking at me, her arms swinging from side to side. I seemed to have gotten her attention now. Just when I was about to squat and talk to her again, a voice screamed from behind.

"Tina! Oh, dear Lord!" a young woman was at her heels towards us. She had the same eyes that Tina had. Eyes that seemed to see through one's heart.

"You've been with my daughter all along? I lost sight of her and I've been searching for her most of the place."

"I saw her looking around, lost and confused and I decided to help her."

"Thank you, I am grateful."

The young woman held her daughter in her arms and walked away. Tina, only looked on from afar with that smile, plastered on her lips. I knew that like Tina, there were so many hungry children in different compartments of the glasshouse, but people were too blind to see the needs of others. Everyone seemed occupied with the menace and disaster flying all around. The glasshouse itself was becoming overpopulated by the tick of the clock. I walked back to meet my parents with a hand in my pocket, brainstorming and wondering if this was truly the beginning of the end.

The birds were tweeting that morning, the sun was smiling fully and even the clouds seemed to be sleeping behind closed doors as there weren't any of them hanging in the sky. It was a quiet morning when the news hit the headlines: The US government had set to implement another operation tagged, " STOP THE FLOOD (STF)." I wasn't too excited as we all didn't know what the operation was all about. Of course, the name, "STOP THE FLOOD" had said it all but no one knew the next line of action that the government wanted to take. Different murmurings had clouded the whole arena where we were because everyone was talking about the STF scheme. I had just finished wearing my sneakers when Dannie's call came in:

"Hey, Katy, what's up? Heard about the STF scheme yet?"

"Yeah, I have. I saw it on the headlines when I woke up" I replied munching on a waffle.

"Oh cool. Let's meet in front of the pet area to talk about it. I'd call the others."

"Alright Dannie, I'd be with you soon."

"See you soon Katy. Make sure to bring along whatever you are eating too" he laughed and hung up.

I smiled as I took another mouthful of waffles. Dannie had a thing for junk food. He could eat a whole room full of them and never get tired. No wonder he had large arms and a protruding tummy. I wrapped some waffles in my bag and planted a kiss on dad's head before running to meet my friends. Dad wasn't bothered about where I went as he knew I was off to meet my friends.

"Hey, buddies. Sorry, I'm late." Dannie, Cassy, Andrew were already waiting for me.

We got down talking but Dannie sure asked about his junk food before we continued.

"So, I don't know what this STF stuff is all about, but I sure hope it makes sense. I'm tired of this creepy glass house." Cassy cried, adjusting her glasses, over and over again while she spoke.

"I think it's got to do with how to put an end to flood like its name says so that we can get out of this place and return to our normal lives. I wonder why we all are still locked up in this damn glasshouse. I mean the flood hasn't gotten to this region yet. It might as well never come at all..."

"I don't think you are correct, Andrew. We shouldn't wait for the flood to come before we take action. imagine if we weren't in this glasshouse and the flood comes visiting, you might as well be better off six feet beneath!" I replied firmly.

"Woah Woah, guys! Cut it out. It's enough. We are here to discuss and not criticize or hurl words at each other. Be cool guys." Dannie intervened.

While we were still talking, Cassy told us to check our phones. She was scouring the web when she got the news that the US government had finally unveiled the full agenda of the STF scheme. The Administrator of Environmental and Ecosystem Affairs had announced that due to the recent population increase in glasshouses, there would be a permanent construction of glass fences around the whole States and coastal cities.

"This would serve as a means for normalcy to return after people return to their homes." the Administrator had stated.

"Yeah! This is fucking cool. Damn! That's what I'm talking about!" Andrew jumped

Those around us were also smiling and talking. Before long, the whole place was already noisy. People were hugging loved ones and friends, glad and happy that we were all going back to our houses after all. Normalcy was finally going to creep into our midst again. I figured that the glasshouses situated in every state were temporary ones. Now, the whole city was going to be fenced with sturdy glass walls that would be able to withstand the torrents of the flood.

Construction of the glass walls started and pictures of it were taken and posted on social media for people to see the progress. They dug deep into the ground such that the glass walls were firmly rooted. They made the construction using huge panels of glass that were seamlessly welded together using the latest technology from a research team from Stanford. This was way bigger than the one we were currently in. It was also bulletproof and had high walls that reached to the sky. It could also withstand extreme temperatures. This made perfect sense. If the whole city was fenced with bulletproof glass, people would be able to live their normal lives without fear of being killed by water or any other thing. Other cities and affected countries had adopted the glass wall strategy too. Within the next few months, I kept myself busy with my research on global warming and how to minimize its impact on us all. I mean since the flood was caused as a result of global warming, I realized that reversing the causes of global warming would reduce the incidence of flooding over time. I informed my buddies about the research and they all took interest in it. Every one of them wanted to help in tackling this environmental menace, Cassy especially. Even Andrew that seemed dubious about it earlier was also in full support now. All hands were on the deck. I was so happy that I was going to leave the glasshouse back to my own house, back to my cozy room, back to my computer and all. I had missed the normalcy.

Three months strolled by and finally, our city had been fortified with the glass walls. Nobody cared that we were living like humans in a fish tank, everyone just wanted to survive. The last three months have been rough and tough because the food was in limited supply. Just when everything was going unbearable, the US government announced that people could return to their houses. Everyone was glad and grateful that they could return to their lives without fear. Even though our region was still in danger of being flooded, I wasn't bothered as I knew that we were ready to face it. We just wished that the wall would withstand the flood. I wonder why the flood hadn't visited our city yet despite its wild exploits and adventure with neighboring cities and states.

Those whose areas that were worst affected by the flood were the ones in lower populated areas. They were to relocate to bigger cities. Coaster buses with the inscription "STF" scheme were provided to transport people and their few belongings, back to their respective destinations. Some people left the glasshouse that very day, without wasting much of the time. My dad and mom were part of the first to vacate the temporal glasshouse we had been in for months. I ran to the pet section to pick Kula up and she was sure happy to see me. The moment I had her fluffy coat in my arms, she bathed my face with her pink tongue. Maybe she also knew that we were leaving the place. Maybe dogs could sense that normalcy was creeping in once again. I leashed her and together, we set off to catch up with mom and dad.

I was going to miss the glasshouse, that was sure. I was going to miss the family that stayed up close to our compartment, a woman, her daughter, and her aged mom. The elderly woman would always smile whenever I waved at her and she would wave both hands at me. I wondered how old she was. I could bet that if she could survive the flood and the glasshouse with all its hustle and bustle, she could as well survive whatever it was that lay before us. I had just gotten out of the glasshouse, together with other families. The STF buses were filling up in no time. Some people were excited to leave the place. Some people were reluctant to leave as they didn't have anywhere to go, so they stayed back. They would be living in a glass house caged in another glasshouse. I was about to enter one of the STF buses when I felt a tug at my skirt. I stood glued to the ground when I realized it was little Tina. She gave me that cute smile of hers and it warmed my heart like it did the first time. I squatted on the side, smiled back, and gave her a bear hug. We were like that for a few seconds before Tina's mom called out to her. She ran off to meet her mom and turned to give me a final wave. Tina and her mom set out to return to the glasshouse then I realized, Tina and her mom were part of those that would not be leaving the glasshouse. They were homeless. For a moment, I stood with my eyes fixed on Tina, wondering what it was like to live on the streets of New York, with blisters all over my body and lice in my hair without a cozy place to call home.

Chapter Three

Home smelt the same. Nothing had changed except for the dust that hung in the air with different sizes of cobwebs hanging around the sitting room. I ran to my bedroom and lay on the bed even though I twitched my nose and sneezed countless times. My room was still the same. My bed was still laid, and my bookshelf was still in shape, with the books in their right places dressed in all shades of dust. The reading table still held my computer and all my writing materials. I smiled as I ran my fingers through my collection of pencils and highlighters lying on the table. It was good to be home again. Kula was barking all over the house and wagging her tail now and then. It was obvious she was happy to be home again. Once I dropped her in her pen, she made circular motions before lying relaxed on her couch. Mom went straight to the kitchen to clean up and started preparing dinner, while dad kept himself busy in his shed, oiling the parts and cleaning his tools. Everyone set out to do a whole round of house cleaning. Normalcy was beginning to creep in on us again.

Businesses that had shut down were gradually reopening again. Malls, grocery stores, markets were beginning to display their goods again. Schools had resumed and I was going for classes every day. Geography remained my favorite subject. Even though I didn't like the wrinkles and creases on Mr. Stanford's face, I was delighted to be in his class again. That day during lunch hour, the cafeteria was filled with different stories of the adventures of the glasshouse that we had all just returned from. The buddies: Cassie, Dannie, Andrew, and I all sat around the same table. We were all talking about how each of us was settling in our homes after the glasshouse experience. Now, that the whole city was fenced with tall glass walls, there was a high degree of safety from the flood to a large extent. But nobody expected the next line of events that ensued in the weeks to come.

I had just kissed mom and dad goodnight on their faces and tucked Kula in her pen. I changed into my pajamas, brushed my teeth, and climbed into my covers with a book in my hand. Few hours before bedtime, I had been reading about recent happenings on the Internet and one of the headlines had stated that even though major cities had been fortified and modified into glass tanks, flooding was still inevitable. The floods were going to visit our region any time soon, we just didn't know when. Natural disasters don't send a signal to prepare you, they'd just arrive and take you unawares. But I wasn't bothered because I was so sure that the high glass cubed walls, built high above sea level were enough to withstand whatever flood that was going to come by.

At exactly 2:00 am, the noise of silence pierced the night, and I woke up. I got out of bed and went to my window. I peeped through and I could see that it wanted to rain. The dark clouds seemed to be boiling with rage, as there were different kinds of flashes racing across the sky. Before I could get back into bed, the whistling noise of the wind had taken over the silence that once prevailed. My curtains were already dancing in free air as the breeze threw them in various directions. I locked the windows carefully and ran under the warmth of my comforter. Lightning and thunder were heard all over the place and I knew that this rain wasn't the usual kind of rain. It hadn't rained for months ever since the flooding events started taking place. I just couldn't imagine the two events, rainfall, and flooding occurring simultaneously. Mom knocked on my door to know If I was safe and I responded with an okay. I had bolted my door and I was too comfy in bed to open the door for mom. "Holy shit! This rainfall was definitely going to increase the sea level again." I muttered to myself as I curled under the comforter.

Maybe this was the way our town had chosen to be flooded. Maybe the rains were the messengers of the flood. What if the rains didn't stop falling and resulted in internal flooding? What if this was the beginning of the end? What if... What if...I kept on asking rhetorically until sleep took the better part of my eyes.

When daylight spread her wings in the morning, the rains were still drizzling, and it didn't look like it was going to stop anytime soon. The whole area was filled with water.

I couldn't believe my eyes. Our car was almost covered with water and the grass that lay on our yard was nowhere to be found. It means there would be no school today, I muttered to myself. Still, in my pajamas, I ran down the steps to see what the news headlines had to say about the morning's downpour. I met dad on the couch.

"Morning dad." I kissed him on his cheek.

"Morning princess. I hope you slept well. It got a little chilly last night."

"I woke up when the weather suddenly changed, but I didn't even know when I slept back. I woke up surprised to see the whole area flooded."

Dad was about to reply to me but the breaking news that ran across the TV screen had caught his attention; "Nonstop rainfall causes temporal flooding in coastal cities."

"Wow, but I thought the glass walls around us were meant to stop the flood from getting in."

"Well, not really, Katy. The glass walls were built around the entire city and around the beaches and lakes to prevent water from getting into the city. It wasn't meant to stop rain in the city. You know the sea level has been on the rise ever since along with rains internally causing the issue, we all have on our hand."

"Hmmm. No one imagined that the rains could also cause internal flooding. I hope it ends soon dad."

I was already on my way upstairs when dad called me to come and see another breaking news with the caption, "The long-awaited flood finally comes around." It was surely an awaited flood because some people had doubted if the floods were real or not, just because we were forced to stay in a safer region. The news correspondent had stated that the morning's rainfall had already increased the sea levels and led to flooding around coastal areas. Dad and I watched on to see if pictures of the flood would be displayed on the screen, but we were only able to see pictures of the glass walls that had been built around the cities. The displayed picture seemed to have been shot from the distance from an overhead drone. I was thankful that the glass walls were already constructed and established before the floods came.

I ran off to my room to call my buddies to talk about the recent happenings. It turned out that Cassy, Andrew, and Dannie were as surprised as I was concerning the persistent rainfall that had occurred and the unexpected flood within our environment. I teased Andrew over the phone and reminded him of the time he mentioned that the floods weren't going to take place. "Well, it turns out that my assumptions were pretty wrong." He replied coldly over the phone.

It was obvious that all activities would be on hold because the streets were flooded and transportation was not feasible. It seemed that normalcy had taken a bow once more. Weeks went by and the rains refused to stop. It wasn't raining violently, the water had reduced to an extent, but the streets were still deserted. No one wanted to be drenched or soaked. I peeped through the window and saw different umbrellas hanging over the heads of different human beings. Schools had closed ever since it started raining nonstop but other people still had to go about their businesses. Those that didn't have cars had to roll their pants up and dip their feet in the muddy waters on the streets. I was thankful that the government had provided the temporal glasshouse we left to house homeless people like little Tina and her mom.

Within the weeks that strolled by, people from less populated towns, and flood survivors of other regions were relocating to the major cities. Those in the countryside that weren't in town began to move and relocate to the glass-walled cities. There were security systems and police forces around the territories of glassed cities to control the influx of people. But as time went on it was uncontrollable and overpopulation became the order of the day. Lesser populated towns were relocating to the big cities and there was little or nothing that the government could do about it. Everyone seemed to be scampering for safety.

The rain reduced to an extent but the whole soil had been clogged with water. The soil seemed to be drunk with rainwater. The flood within the cities reduced, leaving behind a small puddle of muddy waters here and there but at least, people could move around, and schools began to reopen. During the time of the flood, I buried myself in books and of course, listening to the news and keeping up with the weather forecasts. Dad was also keeping up with the news headlines and mom, as usual, kept herself busy with kitchen duties. She would sometimes stay on the couch and knit a woolen coat or two. You could never find mom watching the news. It wasn't her thing.

Three years strolled by and everything took a turn, especially the economy. Food had become an issue. The persistent rainfall that had prevailed in the last three years, had affected farming drastically. Farmlands had become clogged with water and had become too waterlogged to hold any crop. No one planned a long-term survival plan, the first year was a breeze but after three years with millions of people to cater to, things were getting to a rough edge. Fresh crops were out of sight and even the garden at our yard seemed too weak and stressed to produce any green thing. That affected mom and even the way we eat. Mom had planted veggies like lettuce, carrots, broccoli, turnips, cabbage, and other plants for our use but now, the ground was bare. The leftover veggies that were displayed for sale at the grocery store, had their prices hiked because farmers couldn't grow anything at that period.

Farmers began to cry out in their numbers and their protests were all over the news. They were all on the streets with different placards held above their heads, begging the government to intervene. Some placards read, " we are hungry" others read, "help! We need food to survive " and so on. It was so amazing to me that these farmers didn't even mind the fact that their feet had been drenched with mud or that rain was still drizzling or threatening to fall heavier anytime soon.

Economic activities had declined, and cash wasn't regarded as useful anymore. It's like you have money but you can't seem to buy anything with it. Grocery stores were going empty by the day and they weren't getting stocked again. Canned foods weren't even in sight at all. I didn't know the extent to which we had run in short supplies on food in the garage until the day we gathered at the table for dinner and I saw what was served; mashed potatoes and eggs.

"Mom, where are the veggies? I thought you went to the grocery store today."

"yes, I did honey. But there wasn't anything to buy. The grocery store seemed virtually empty."

"well, I guess we'd just make do with what we have now and hope that things get better," Dad replied with his mouth full.

I slowly ate my potatoes but picked at the eggs on my plate. Things were beginning to get ugly and it seemed like we were in for a temporary famine. I was sad as I couldn't do anything to help the situation and my heart was bleeding. I had read a whole lot about geography, agriculture, and farming. Yet, there was little or nothing that I could do. I was lost in thoughts again until Kula's slow whims brought me back to reality and she curled below my feet. She was also hungry, and her Dog food was going to finish any moment. "There has got to be a way out. This whole fucking crisis must come to an end." I whispered to myself and continued picking at my plate.

The US government had set up an emergency committee to look into the food crisis that had encroached on the States. Those individuals who had large storehouses filled with food became the most wanted and respected in the community. Some of them began to distribute food to smaller towns and communities as a means of helping in their own way. The STF buses also began to distribute relief materials to poverty-stricken regions to provide food. There were a lot of hungry mouths to feed and there were limited hands, so there came a call for volunteers to help. As soon as the call for volunteer's ad came out, I chatted with my buddies. I had already created a group page and called it "DACK against the Flood" (Dannie, Andrew, Cassy, and Katy). We were meant to hang out and discuss physically, but the streets weren't so safe because of protests and social unrest. Cassy's message was the first to beep on my phone and the other guys followed suit. They all agreed to join the volunteers that would provide food for hungry people.

DACK amidst other young individuals became registered members of the STF scheme and we were given vests with the inscription, STF boldly written in large white letters across the front of the red vest. We were also given black rubber boots to be able to walk through the mud on the ground. There were hundreds of STF buses scattered along the streets of each state to supply relief materials to hungry people. For the first time in forever, I felt this peace and joy within that I was making a difference on the ground. Cassy also felt the same, I saw a radiant smile plastered on her face while she delivered food to hungry homes.

One of the places we supplied food to, was the temporary glasshouse where we were housed before. I was so happy to visit that place again. It held memories of the time we had spent there. The first thing I did when we arrived in front of the glasshouse was to run my fingers in circular motions around the glass walls. It was fun! The place was densely populated, filled with people who had relocated from flood-prone areas, less populated cities, and those who were homeless. While we distributed the materials, my eyes roamed around the vicinity to see if I could sight Tina or her mom. I had missed the little girl and my soul seemed drawn to her in a way that I couldn't explain. Maybe it was because she made me feel like an older sister when I held her in my arms or because her hazel-colored eyes seemed to see through my soul and calm the turbulent floods of unrest within my heart. My hands continued to distribute while my eyes roamed about, looking like it had lost a priceless treasure.

We returned to our homes when the sun settled behind the clouds and each volunteer was given a pack of cereals, grains, eggs, potatoes, noodles, greens, and oranges to also share with our families. We were also given a pack of chocolates that made Dannie super hyper. We all stopped in front of our homes, I got out of the bus, waved back at the people still in it, and walked inside the house. Cassy,

Dannie, and Andrew had already gotten to their homes too. My hands were tired and weary. I got rid of my already soiled boots outside before stepping into the house. Mom and dad were sitting on the couch and I hugged them both before running upstairs to take a shower.

"Hope you had fun honey."

"Yes, I sure did mom. I'm just too tired!" I screamed from my bedroom as I undressed to go take a hot bath.

While I lay on the bed to sleep that night, my face was lit with a smile as I switched off the lamp by my bed. Two things made me smile. First, my buddies and I were able to help with the flood and famine crisis. Second, I have seen Tina that day: after reaching out to give a man with a face sprinkled with pimples a pack, I felt a tug on my shorts, and I didn't have to look down before I knew that it was Tina. I squatted and held her in my arms for what passed for some minutes. She held me in return and smiled. When I had hugged her to my heart's content, I let her down on the floor and gave her a little care package for kids. I also gave her two bars of Snickers. She danced around and dashed off. I stood transfixed wondering why she ran off not until she reappeared again with her mom. I hugged her mom and gave her a package too. She smiled in return with that same spark lit in her eyes like Tina's. She made to go before she warmly held my hands and whispered gently into my ears.

"Thanks for coming to see Tina. She's been mute right from when she lost her dad, but ever since she met you, she's been able to make some audible sounds and also laugh when she's playing. That means a whole lot to me. Thank you, miss..."

"Katy. The name's Katy." I replied before hugging her again.

That was the last memory I had that night before sleep took over my eyes. That night was a special kind of night, devoid of nightmares and wandering thoughts.

Chapter Four

Things had started to go south again. The government couldn't keep up with the increasing population and the STF buses were soon running out of supplies. I figured that if the food was being distributed from large warehouses and not replaced, the whole community would soon run out of supplies, and that's exactly what was beginning to happen. Social unrest had returned to the streets again. Some people were going from house to house begging for donations. I wondered how the homeless people in the first glasshouse were faring. I wondered if they had anything to eat too. Farmers took to the streets again, protesting and canvassing for government intervention. The whole situation seemed messy. I mean we were all caged in a glass cubed city like fish in glass tanks, outside the glass tanks there were floods and sea levels are rising by the minute. No one could go out or come in. It seemed like we all were trapped.

"Common guys, there has got to be a way out. We gotta figure this whole thing out." I told the buddies when we sat around the park in our estate.

"Maybe if we come up with a reasonable idea, we could sell it to the government or even the STF scheme since we are a part of them now. What do y'all think?" Cassy replied adjusting her glasses now and then.

The guys, Andrew and Dannie seemed rather too quiet to talk or make any comments. While we sat, different groups of farmers walked past. All with equipment and boots of various kinds to navigate their movements through the sticky ground. Some of them looked really hungry and pale. Hunger had beaten the entire state once more. And this time, it was not a joke anymore.

When the protests seemed to increase by the day, the government decided to have a closed-door meeting with farmers in the area, regarding the way forward in tackling the issue of the clogged soil and sought out means of increasing the fertility level again to improve farming efficiency. No one knew what was discussed that day until the news headlines said what was conversed behind closed doors.

"The US government had just concluded the closed-door meeting with some of the farmer groups in the country. The meeting was meant to provide a way forward for reducing the social unrest of hunger in society, also to discuss ways of improving and enhancing the soil's fertility. The meeting didn't draw into a fruitful conclusion, but the US government had assured farmers that adequate measures would be taken in ensuring that hunger was fought in our midst." Well, that is the news for today and I am Shaine Stone reporting.

I switched off the TV and was amazed to see mom peeping from the kitchen. She seemed to have been listening to the news all along.

"Mom, really? You were watching the news all along?" I asked her amidst bursts of laughter.

"Cut it out, Katy." She replied with a scrunch on her face. "I'm really concerned about the situation around. I mean, food is scarce now baby. The government has to do something, else we all would probably starve to death. So, I had to see what the news had to say."

"I know you are concerned mom. I'm also concerned too but things would come around. I'm pretty sure the government would intervene pretty soon. But I was just so thrilled to see your eyes glued to the news. Dad and I know you never like listening to the news update." I replied laughing again. Mom just smiled back at me and returned to the kitchen. I switched off the TV and hurried to my room. I had a broad smile spread across my face because I had seen mom interested in the news, and I was going to let dad know when he arrived.

Sunrise and sunsets passed, and nothing seemed to have changed. But while surfing the Internet one cool morning, I came across a young group of farmers. They seemed to be between their mid-twenties and thirties. They had come out in their numbers to educate citizens and other fellow farmers about the greenhouses. I was elated when I later discovered that these young groups of farmers were going to hold and host awareness campaigns and peaceful assemblies, to educate the entire public about greenhouses and how it could tackle the situation of hunger hanging around.

A young woman was the leader of the Young Farmers Union and she led a peaceful campaign across the streets telling people about the greenhouses. She was going to host a major campaign in our city, and I was elated. I wanted to be a part of the program and possibly help in volunteering as I did with the STF scheme. The US government had also partnered with these young team of farmers and had promised to assist in empowering farmers all over with whatever materials they needed in establishing greenhouses. The morning of the campaign did come, but with a string of sickness too. I woke up feeling weak and my head felt like it couldn't stay on my neck.

"Oh! Damn it! I planned to attend today's program." I murmured under my covers amidst body aches. There was a feverish feeling. Mom came to wake me up and saw that I was shivering. She sped to get a thermometer. By the time it had stayed for some time in my mouth, my temperature read 102.5 degrees Fahrenheit. I knew that I wasn't going to step my foot out of the house for the rest of that day. I managed to put a call through to the buddies to tell them to either join the ongoing campaign or watch it on TV as I intended to do. It was only Dannie that responded. I left a voice message for Andrew and Cassy.

"Ain't you gonna join the campaign, Katy. It looks like it's gonna be a lot of fun. Plus, I heard there would be free candies distributed at the end of the program."

" I am under the weather, Dannie. But I'll try to keep up with the live broadcast on TV." I replied faintly.

" Awwww, Katy. Get well soon girl. You'd come around, okay? Got to go now and catch up with Andrew and Cassy... Get well soon girl."

Mom brewed a hot cup of coffee as I curled up on the couch to watch the Television. If I wasn't going to be physically present in the program, I was going to follow every bit of the program on TV. The young female farmer who headed the campaign looked like she is in her mid-twenties. She had a firm way of talking when she held the microphone. I loved her courageous spirit. I took note of her name, Brenda Scout, and decided that I was going to google her profile.

"The greenhouse effect is a natural process that warms the earth's surface when the sun's energy reaches the earth's atmosphere and keeping it warm enough to sustain life. Some of it is reflected back to space and the rest is absorbed and re-radiated by greenhouse gases." She continued,

"Human activities such as burning fossil fuels, agriculture, and land clearing are increasing the number of greenhouse gases released into the atmosphere. Greenhouse gases include water vapor, carbon dioxide, methane, nitrous oxide, ozone, and some artificial chemicals such as CFCs."

I smiled all through the time I was listening to Brenda talk and educate fellow farmers on what the greenhouse effect was all about and how the greenhouses could be constructed. I had read about it many times and I was glad that the awareness was finally coming to the limelight. Maybe this would be a way out of the hunger menace. While the program was going on, different elderly farmers began to ask different questions ranging from how greenhouses could be constructed to how it could be maintained and what plants could be grown in them. The young lady called up her partner on stage, a young curly blond-haired guy, about the same age as her. He went on to explain that the commercial greenhouses could be constructed to grow crops that could feed the entire population. He also said that greenhouses could also be constructed to raise and grow crops. He also added that greenhouse crops are usually protected from field pests and other plant diseases.

"What kind of plants can be grown in a greenhouse," an elderly woman with a hat stood up to ask the question.

"Oh, a lot of plants can be grown in a greenhouse. Geraniums, impatiens, salvia, caladiums, ferns, auberges. You can also produce crops that don't do well outside such as Cucumbers and lettuce, salad mix, and maximize profits too." The young man replied, and farmers were already smiling on their seats. He later went on to itemize the different crops that could be grown in different seasons.

"But there are different crops that can grow per season. Peppers and chilies, tomatoes, can grow all through the summer months. The fall sun is perfect weather for raising late salad crops, Calabrese, and French beans. Winter vegetables could also be grown in the cold season. Okra, melons, sweet potatoes could grow in the greenhouses too."

The equipment needed for keeping the greenhouses in perfect condition was also stated such as screening installation, heating and cooling systems, lighting, and probably a computing system to optimize conditions for plant growth. The program was gradually coming to an end and farmers were elated that there was finally going to be a way out. Brenda was about to give her last speech when I saw Dannie raise his hand to ask a question. I wasn't too amazed to see him ask a question. Dannie was a curious lad, and he wasn't shy to satisfy his curiosity no matter what it took.

"How many days does it take to construct a greenhouse miss?"

"Well, it could take two to three days to assemble a normal or standard greenhouse," Brenda replied Dannie with a smile. I could see Cassy and Andrew shaking their heads and giggling while Dannie sat down. I really wished that I was with the buddies but watching the TV and following all the events of the program from home, wasn't such a bad idea after all. After taking some medications and a bowl of hot soup, I drifted to sleep on the couch.

The construction of greenhouses began a few days after the program was held. Different greenhouses were being erected in different parts of the States. Some greenhouses were Lean-To, Even-Span and some were built in the Gothic-arch style. I could identify and name most of the greenhouses that were being displayed on the news because I had seen pictures of them before. The government had granted loans to farmers as a means of empowering them to start up their own greenhouses. Various commercial greenhouses that were worth thousands of dollars were erected in strategic portions of the state too. Experts in the field were put in charge of the management of the commercial side of things. Commercial greenhouses would be connected by underground pipes to the exterior of the city so that some of the stagnant flooded water would travel through the pipes to serve as a source of water to the large portion of crops. Fruits, flowers, and other major vegetables were going to be grown in the commercial greenhouses.

Some rich folks and other wealthy farmers had converted their backyards and courtyards into mini-greenhouses to grow foods of their choice. I was particularly excited as I knew I was going to see a real greenhouse soon, especially because some individuals in our state had started constructing theirs. All the greenhouses I had seen were pictures on the Internet and some other ones that were displayed in the textbooks. Mr. Stanford had told us at different times in his classes, that he had a square foot free-standing greenhouse at the rear of his house and I always hoped that I would be able to see it one day. But now I was not going to wait any longer. Greenhouses were springing forth all around.

A retired couple was living a few blocks away from ours, Mr. and Mrs. Bryan. I had always waved at them whenever I was taking a walk with Kula or riding on my bike during summers. But ever since the grounds and roads got messy with puddles and sticky mud, I had been indoors most of the day. Even though the rains had reduced to a minimal level and the roads were a tad more improved, I wasn't still going out as I used to. But one particular evening, I decided to take a stroll around to see if I was going to see any greenhouses around the neighborhood. I had not gone too far when I noticed Bryan's house. I realized that their car garage was being modified into a greenhouse. They were constructing a greenhouse. Woah! I ran off to meet Mrs. Bryan mowing her lawn. Mrs. Bryan had a smile that could melt any cold heart, even though she seemed stricken with age. Her smile seemed ever-youthful.

"Hello, Mrs. Bryan. May I lend you a hand?'

"Oh, dear! I'd be delighted, Katy. You know I don't get by to see youngsters like you around most of these days. Thank you, Katy," she replied and flashed a heartwarming smile of hers my way. I didn't really know much about the elderly couple, but I did know that they were kind and Mrs. Bryan baked the best homemade pies I had ever tasted in my entire life. She always made to share her pies with us during Thanksgiving.

I asked Mrs. Bryan about the greenhouse they were constructing. She went on with the details of the greenhouse, the type of crops they intended to grow, and how they were going to sell off some of the produce to grocery stores around the vicinity.

When she was done mowing, Mrs. Bryan took me to where the greenhouse was and showed me around. There were a couple of guys working on the greenhouse with Mr. Bryan. One of the men had Mr. Bryan's kind of straight nose and I needed no soothsayer to tell me he was Mr. Bryan's son. It was a magnificent building, even though the work wasn't done yet. The glass walls made me remember the first glasshouse where we had stayed before.

The greenhouse was built in the shape of a rectangle it was 13 feet tall and its roof was made of Solexx twin-walled covering as Mr. Bryan had explained. He also told me he had decided to make it into a rectangular shape to trap midday heat when the sun was shining on its broad south-facing surface. I saw another room filled with greenhouse equipment like coolers, heaters, ventilators, and other systems to control the temperature and environmental conditions of the greenhouse. Mr. Bryan also said he intended to make a section of the greenhouse a hothouse to grow special root crops and plants. I stood in amazement as I looked around. I was finally in a greenhouse! I couldn't wait to tell Cassy, Dannie, and Andrew about the greenhouse I had seen.

I thanked Mr. Bryan and he told me that I could come to check out the place from time to time whenever I wanted to. Before leaving the house, Mrs. Bryan gave me a cup of freshly squeezed lemonade. After one gulp, I realized how much I had missed lemonades. I gave Mrs. Bryan a warm hug before leaving the house. I walked back home for dinner with a huge smile plastered on my face. I was going to pen it down in my diary that I had seen a greenhouse directly for the first time.

By the end of the coming week, different glasshouses and hothouses had been built in several places.

Chapter Five

"If we fall, we fall together and if we rise, we rise together."
I had heard that phrase in a song while going for evening
strolls with my earphones on and that phrase had come to
stick with me. I wrote it on each page of my sticky note
and had some of them stuck around my dresser's mirror. I
would always see it boldly written when I stood to brush
my hair or stare at my image in the mirror. I realized that
the flood had brought with it, a kind of unity and bond that
tied different people together. At least, it had brought
farmers from different cities together, to fight with one
voice and the idea of widespread greenhouses had come
out of it. Now, various and diverse greenhouses were
springing forth around, flourishing and blooming. Some
farmers were even helping others to construct theirs. It
was all beginning to make sense. Everyone had realized
that the floods, the food crisis, and homelessness were a
common enemy. Together we were all going to fight. No
one knew what the future held or when the waters were
going to go down, but we all knew that we all got to survive
against all odds.

I had just returned from the STF volunteers team hangout. We met to know each other better, played some games, discussed and shared ideas about ways we could improve the needs of the neighborhood and the city. I got back weary and tired as a bee. Mom and dad had earlier told me they would be going for a walk, so I had the whole house to myself and Kula. The dog jumped on me, licking and sniffing my face at the same time. I patted its head with my eyes half open, wondering why mom and dad hadn't taken Kula along with them. When Kula was gone, I stretched out on the sofa and closed my eyes, my hands dabbing the front of my head. I lay there immersing myself in the silence. Out of nowhere, I heard what sounded like a mini-explosion with great intensity. Alarmed, I got up from the sofa and realized that there was a power outage. At this point, every drop of sleep in my eyes had been wrung out completely. I hurried up the stairs and turned the doorknob of my room, unlocked it, and switched on the light bulbs. There was no flicker of light and even my computer is off. I stood there, somewhat glued to the ground before Dad's incoming call made me blink.

"Hello, Katy. Where are you? Are you home? Are you alright?" He asked amidst heavy breathing.

"I am fine, dad. I came home a few minutes ago. Dad, did you hear that loud noise?"

"Yes, I did, we both did hear it and that's why I called to make sure you are safe. We are on our way back. We will soon be at home."

"Alright, dad." I hung up and walked around my room, my mind wandering in a million paths. Ever since I could hold a doll, I never experienced a power outage of any sort, but the event of the last few minutes had changed the status quo of things. I ran down the stairs and returned to the sofa, waiting for mom and dad to return.

Mom and dad arrived briefly ten minutes later, with sweat beads sitting on the pores of their foreheads and arms. Mom waved at me before running upstairs to take a shower. Dad took a seat by my side and had already held the remote in his hands, before realizing that there was no power. I giggled in my seat. Dad had gotten used to the TV. I wondered how he was going to survive this power outage. Dad told me he wasn't very much surprised to see that there was a power outage, because of the intensity of the noise.

We still had a small quantity of petrol in the garage and dad made do with it and emptied the contents of the gas into the generator. We hadn't used the generator in years, and I was surprised when its engine coughed and roared to life when dad turned it on. I had just a little battery left on my phone. I walked to my room to charge my phone. Dad instantly turned on the TV to see what the headlines had to say about the power outage. I rushed downstairs and sat next to dad on the sofa, while the news correspondent went on with the news.

There was a national power outage, it was said to have occurred at the same time when I have heard the noise earlier in the day. No one knew for sure what the exact cause of the power outage was, but some geology experts had stated that the rising floods and sea levels might have affected above-ground and underground electrical equipment and probably destroyed the entire power infrastructure of the country. Mom joined us much later, on the sofa, with a towel tied around her hair. She seemed interested in the news, she realized that there was going to be a total blackout.

The sun was already going to bed and darkness began to creep in on the whole nation. The generator had stopped breathing, a few minutes after the news ended and the whole world fell silent. The darkness that hung around seemed unusual and weird. I switched on my phone's light to ease the tension of the prevailing darkness. We had a few candles that had been tucked away in the kitchen drawers. Mom brought out large white candles from the kitchen. I lit it, dripped a little wax into a plate, and stood it up. Thankfully, the moonlight seemed bright that night. Mom, Dad, and I sat facing the candle amid the hushed surroundings.

The still shadows of the moonlight and the swaying motion of the shadows of the candlelight met and conflated on the walls of the sitting room. Kula was heard whimpering in her pen. I knew that she was aware that there was a power outage. When there was nothing more to talk about, I kissed mom and dad goodnight, walked towards my bedroom with my phone's light guiding me through. That night, sleep seemed like it had left my eyes for a long time. I couldn't close my eyes. Everywhere was quiet and calm. But steaming in through the windows, the moonlight cast long shadows and splashed the walls of my room with a tint of pale colors. I hadn't seen such a bright moon for years. Sleep finally found its way into my eyes and the last thing I saw was the soft tufts of white glow dancing on the walls of my room.

The following day at school, everyone was talking about the power outage that had occurred the night before. Even our science teacher had talked about the power outage while she taught that morning. Dannie had asked a lot of questions that morning and Miss Stephanie, the science teacher was bored and fed up with Dannie's questions. She called the class to a close even before the change of class bell was rung. During the break, the buddies and I had sat at our usual table to eat. We had fried fish with a green salad, boiled vegetables, and rice for lunch. Ever since the inception of the greenhouses, there had been a lot of vegetables and fruits around. Even the school had introduced vegetables as a predominant part of the lunch menu. Andrew had just set aside a fishbone on his plate when he threw a question at Dannie.

"You seemed to have come with a box full of questions for Miss Stephanie today. You just kept on asking loads and loads of questions, dude. I got bored at a point you know."

"Well, I had to ask her questions about the power outage. Physics and electricity have a lot in common." Dannie replied with his mouth full of rice.

"No kidding guys, this power outage is a big deal. I mean I stayed awake most of the night because of the darkness hanging around. I haven't seen this kind of stuff take place my whole life." Cassy replied carefully wiping the lens of her glasses with a cloth. She went on,

" I'm concerned and tired of everything. First, it was the flood that came unannounced, then we had to move to a temporary glasshouse, then greenhouses are everywhere and now this! When would all this stop? I'm sick and tired." She replied with a somber expression on her face.

I finished eating the last grain of rice on my plate and dabbed at the corners of my mouth before speaking out.

"Okay guys, for real, I'm as puzzled and surprised as we all are about the power outage and all. But we gotta think of something. You know we've been through one hurdle or the other and somehow, we all smuggle ourselves out of it. This is another hurdle and I believe we all gonna jump over it in no time. But there has to be a way out." I responded with a crumple on my face.

We went on talking about the power outage and the effect it would have on a lot of things; productivity would reduce, the health sector was going to suffer, and some lives might be lost, there might be limitations to the use of internet facilities and so much more. I couldn't use my computer or my phone anymore and it started affecting me. I mean, how was I going to survive days without the internet? It made me feel like I was sort of cut off from the entire world. I overheard a black girl, about the same age as myself. It was said that one could tell the age of a person, by the sound of his or her voice. She was talking from behind. She was on the table behind our table and though I didn't turn to look at her, I could infer from her voice that she was sobbing. She was saying that her mom was ill at the hospital and was placed on life support. She was scared that the power outage would make her mom stop breathing and just cross over to the other side of death. At this point, I turned to steal a glance at them, and I could see the shoulders of the girl move up and down with grief. A lot of lives were surely going to go down. That was inevitable.

My nightmares soon returned. I thought I had gotten over them, but they didn't seem to have gotten over me. Ever since the power outage, I always found my eyes wide open like a bright ray of torchlight in the night. Whenever I dreamt, I still saw water all over me. But it wasn't just the water this time, I seemed to be lost in the grip of darkness too. I would always wake up in the pool of my sweat. "I can't just wait for all these to be over." I cried aloud when I woke up the next morning. By the time I looked up myself in the mirror, there were dark shadows under my eyes, like I had been starved of sleep for days.

Weeks rolled up into months and the prices of gasoline had tripled. Many people had been accustomed to buying gasoline to run their generators as a means of an alternative, temporary power supply but gasoline was awfully expensive. Some other people who could not afford started moving into the glasshouses again, where the government was able to provide electricity for basic needs. Dad couldn't do without the news and so he opted for gasoline to power our generator, amid the hike in price. There was an increase in the social unrest of citizens again.

The American Electric Power (AEP) had also stated during a press conference on the news that they had never experienced this kind of power outage ever since the company began to supply electricity to over a million citizens. They however stated that they were going to keep on with their research of alternate means to generate electricity and restore the power grid. I had read about electricity being generated from about sixty-three percent from fossil fuels, coal, natural gas, petroleum, and other gases while twenty percent was from nuclear energy and about eighteen percent was from renewable sources of energy. But now, gasoline and petroleum were in extremely limited supply and the ones available were very expensive. I wondered how the AEP was going to tackle the present situation but that didn't stop me from reading. Dad had begun to buy The New Yorker and that served as a daily source of information when we couldn't access the internet or when we ran short of gasoline. Bicycles were seen more on the streets now. Gasoline shortage had reduced the number of cars that roamed the streets.

Soon, everyone realized that each city had to be self-sufficient. The sea levels were still prevailing, there is not much that the government or AEP could do. The floods had come to stay. We all had to find a way to survive. Darkness became the norm and I had gotten used to it. I could even walk down the stairs from my bedroom to the sitting room without missing a step. Some nights we burned the candles and other nights, we turned on the generator whenever we had to listen to the news update.

The intensity and frequency of dad's voice traveled from the sitting room, through the stairs, into my bedroom, and finally took a halt in my eardrum, ringing incessantly until my eyes sat open.

"Daaaaaaad. Why are you yelling? It's Saturday for heaven's sake!" I screamed from my room with my eyes still drowsy.

"Sorry, sweetie but you gotta come, see this now."

I covered myself with the comforter and placed my pillows atop my head. I had been awake most of the night. I wasn't ready to have another round of nightmares. But sleep finally came around 3 A.M. I was sleeping peacefully until his loud voice pulled me up. I wanted to sleep all day.

"Katy, I'm waiting. You don't wanna miss this news."

I hesitated before I dragged my body up from the bed, went down the stairs to see dad.

"Katy what in the world! You look like you haven't slept in ages. Now you got eye bags dancing all-around your eyes."

"Morning dad. What's up?"

He closed his eyes before replying," they've finally found a way to restore the power."

I screamed and ran to hug dad, jumping and yelling wide with ecstasy.

"How did you come about the news dad?"

"Well, I got the New Yorker and that was what the headlines had to say." I collected the newspaper from dad and read what its content had to say. A manufacturing firm in Nebraska had been relying solely on solar power, ever since the inception of the firm. They didn't have to suffer from the general power outage, and so while most of the nation was wallowing in darkness, they weren't affected a bit. They developed redundant systems and technology that would efficiently harvest solar power. They have a few ideas and suggestions to help the US government adopt technology at a rapid pace. The idea is to spread solar energy into most of the US towns. The US government together with the AEP then decided to help cities adapt. They started providing an adequate number of solar panels and systems necessary to go completely Solar. Solar systems were going to be installed in huge fields to generate power. Each field would generate the amount of solar energy required to power the electricity needs of the whole city. That meant each city would be self-sufficient with its power needs with the help of its own environment. This essentially decentralizes our power grid, so even if one area gets affected by the power outage it won't cause a domino effect and affect more localities. I finished reading the whole page of the power outage news, my eyes skimming through each line like they were being followed.

"What's all the yelling about? I could hear your two voices right from the yard." Mom asked with a harvest of greens in her hands. I figured she had just returned from Bryan's greenhouse, as was her routine every Saturday morning these days. They had told mom to come and get fresh vegetables from their greenhouse whenever she needed them.

"We finally have a solution to the power outage. Solar systems would be generating energy for each city." I answered mom still beaming with smiles.

Mom began her episode of yelling. Dad and I laughed while we watched her skipping here and there. We all were excited and that was a beautiful way to start a Saturday morning. By the time I took the stairs and went back to my room, sleep had deserted my eyes. I picked up my cell phone, thankful it still had some battery left in it and I dialed the buddies. I wanted to know if they had heard the good news.

By the following week, the STF scheme had begun to distribute solar panels and systems around the country. My buddies and I were part of the distribution. Every volunteer had been briefed about the systems and how they could be installed. Each house was going to have a solar panel installed on its roof in addition to the power generated in the field. During the day, the light would be converted into power with the help of photovoltaic cells in the solar panels. The Solar panels installed on the roof would then generate Direct Current (DC). This is then fed into a solar inverter which converts the DC from the solar panels into an

Alternating Current (AC) that we use to power our houses. We had helped some houses to install their solar panels and it was a whole lot of fun. I met different people, little boys, and girls that reminded me of Tina. Their smiles warmed my heart like Tina's. This time, it was another team of STF volunteers that had gone to install solar panels in the glasshouse for the homeless. Some smaller communities that were not too far from each other, all shared solar panels that were installed on fields nearby, I realized that each city was now generating its own source of power. Well, the AEP might not be functional until the floods dried, but I knew that wasn't going to happen anytime soon. Even if the floods do go down, each city was already running and surviving on its own.

Chapter Six

The sun was at its zenith when the first airplane crashed into the park nearby. It was a very loud noise, and I could hear it from my room. I had just returned from school that day, and I had a splitting headache. I came home and met dad on the roof of the house, trying to install an extra solar panel.

"Hi, dad. Why in the world are you adding another solar panel? Ain't the once we have enough?" I asked, squinting my eyes to look up, with one hand shielding my face from the sun's fury. The sun's rays were at their peak and looked like they were threatening to blind my eyes.

"Well, Katy. It's just so we could have enough power in the house. More so, it's cool to have another source of power in case the efficiency on the other one decreases. Now, why don't you go inside and have a cool bath huh? The weather seems unfriendly today. "Dad replied wiping beads of sweat off his neck. Dad was a hard worker and loved to do things by himself like painting the house, fixing gadgets, and appliances. Mom was preparing lunch and she kissed me on the cheek when I walked in.

"Hey, mom."

"Hey, Katy. You look tired and spent. Come on, go wash up, and come have some lunch. It would be ready before you are done in the shower." Mom replied with a little smile on her face. I quietly walked up the stairs, my head heavy with every step I took. I just wanted to sleep all evening. We had a pop quiz at school and the surprise of the test, left me with a headache all day. I told Cassy that I was going to sleep all evening immediately after I got home. But that didn't look feasible anytime soon. I had just come out of the bathroom when I heard the plunk of the crash. I hurriedly entered a skirt laid out on my bed, wore a blouse, and ran downstairs. At that point, I already forgot that I had a headache. I ran outside to meet mom and other neighbors in the hood outside. Everyone had a wrinkle of fright and surprise all over their faces. Dad was still on the roof and was squinting to see ahead. I wondered what he was trying to look at so keenly,

"Dad, won't you come down? It's not safe up there, you heard the noise!" I shouted with both hands cupped around the corners of my mouth. Dad didn't seem to pay any attention to me. He just kept on stretching and trying to look ahead. Some neighbors were already staring at him, wondering why he was still up there.

"Honey, would you please come down, now! Do you want your head blown off or something? You heard the noise, please come down now!" Mom yelled at dad. She was still holding a spoon in her hand. It was obvious she just ran out of the kitchen. It was after mom spoke that dad exclaimed from the roof,

"It's a crash y'all! A plane just crashed into the open space in the park. I was trying to see." Dad replied as he was coming down from the roof. By the time he was by my side, a heavy thick mass of smoke was in the air. All three of us went back into the house while some people on the street kept on looking at the smoke hanging in the distance. I was peeping from the window, trying to steal a glance from the distance. I wondered what the airplane was carrying, and I hoped that no life had been lost. Dad didn't even take off his shoes before he turned the TV on. I was eager to see what the news had to say. Even mom was sitting on the sofa, keen to know what the news had to say. As soon as the TV came on, the news headlines were in bold letters, staring back at me in the face:

STF Relief Airplane Crashes into Saint Lukas Park."

The news correspondent had more to say.

"About a few minutes ago, one of the STF relief airplanes crashed into the center of the Saint Lukas Park. The airplane was carrying tons of frozen food that are supposed to be supplied to local communities and stores. The plane didn't immediately start burning when it crashed, but it suddenly exploded when some people were trying to save some of the plane's goods. Ten people were killed, including the pilot and the crew. More news to come later in the day. I am Walter Blanc, reporting live."

The pictures of the burning plane and smoke and screams around the scene of the crash remained glued to my memory for the rest of the evening. I couldn't stop thinking about the crash scene displayed on the television. I still remembered the charred pieces of the plane and the remains of burnt people wrapped in black bin wrappers. It was after I watched the news, my head split with pain again.

That night as I lay on my bed, all I could see were pictures of the burning plane. Of course, I knew that the remains of humans were also part of the fire. The headache was acute, and I thought I was going to be sick all night. I had lost my appetite for food, but mom made sure I took a bowl of soup before going to bed. She also gave me some painkillers when she noticed a frown on my face. The headache did subside but had now returned as I lay beneath my covers. I dreamt that night and all I could see in my dreams were burning airplanes and charred remains of humans everywhere I went.

Ever since the floods and rising sea levels, fishing had become an impossible task because of the torrents and waves. There was a ban that no fishing activities would ensue until the waters had returned to normal sea level. Airplanes had been bringing in frozen foods from other states and supplying them to local communities and stores. The prices of frozen foods had been hiked too because of the transportation costs, but it was still affordable. This plane crash was the first of its kind ever since the transportation of frozen foods has begun. Now that the crash had occurred and taken several lives with it, I wondered whether such a routine would continue.

The news of the crash was the talk of the moment when we arrived at school the next day. We were all talking about it before the first teacher came to class. When the teacher was about to start the class, I noticed Ashley, the blonde, freckled girl that sat right in front of me in class, was absent. I wouldn't have been worried if any other person had been absent from school, but Ashley never skipped school and was always very punctual. She had won awards for the most punctual student for three consecutive years. Why wasn't she at school? My mind began to wander in a million directions. I paid half attention in class all through that morning, while I hoped that Ashley was safe and sound.

"Well, I was grateful that I wasn't in the park yesterday taking my usual evening walks," Dannie replied with a burger in between his teeth.

"The crash wasn't expected at all. I mean all this while, planes have been flying in and out of the states at least once every week, distributing supplies that weren't within our reach. No one ever thought a crash would occur anytime soon." Andrew replied.

I was quiet all through while Andrew and Dannie conversed. Cassy had gone to the restroom since the last class ended and had not returned since then. I wondered what had kept her in there for so long.

"Katy, what's wrong? You've barely said a word since we came here, and your burger seems cold already. What's up?" Andrew asked with concern written all over his face. I was about to reply when Cassy appeared looking all stressed and weak.

"Where have you been all day? You got me freaking out you know." I asked Cassy.

"I've been in the restroom. It took a little longer than usual. Nothing to worry about. Sorry for keeping y'all all worried. So, what did I miss?" Cassy said dabbing her face with a towel.

" I've been worried sick about Ashley. She never misses school and She's always punctual. What could have gone wrong? I have a hunch she ain't safe." I replied with a somber expression on my face. Cassy also seemed concerned about Ashley too, but the guys were buried in their conversation about the crash and what might happen after. Dannie even asked if he could eat up my burger since I wasn't interested, and I gave it to him. He didn't even hesitate before he began to eat up voraciously. I figured hamburgers were his favorite.

Cassy and I were still talking about Ashley's absence when Mrs. Helen, our class teacher walked into the cafeteria with her eyes drunk with tears. She tried to compose herself, but her shaky voice gave her away.

"Hello everyone. You all know that there was a plane crash yesterday. Well, we would be going over to Ashley's place any moment from now. We would need ten volunteers to go visit Ashley. Her dad was among the crew that died yesterday in the crash. We need five girls and five boys. Who's in?"

Of course, DACK had their hands up immediately after Mrs. Helen finished the announcement. Other students who had their hands up were also selected to make a total of ten pupils. We were all going to go to our respective homes after we left Ashley's house. I heaved a sigh of relief when Mrs. Helen made it clear that it was Ashley's dad that died and Ashley was safe. I saw Mrs. Helen wiping a tear from her eyes, I thought it was Ashley who died. Ashley and I weren't the best of friends, but she had a sweet character that seemed to rub off on those around her, including me. Whenever I was quiet or lost in thoughts, Ashley would always seem to understand and flash a smile at me. She was a caring soul. I couldn't bear the thought of losing her or the beauty of her smile. Merely thinking about her dying sent cold shivers down my spine.

We set off to go visit Ashley together with Mrs. Helen and two other teachers. I was a lot better when we got on the bus. Cassy sat right beside me wiping her glasses every now and then. I wondered whether she never got tired of wiping those thick lenses of her. When we got to Ashley's house, it all made perfect sense why Mrs. Helen was crying when she got to the cafeteria to give the announcement. Mrs. Helen was Ashley's aunt.

The US government had given strict bans on the aviation sector after the plane crash occurred. They had stated that it wasn't safe to fly airplanes again because of the harsh weather conditions. They just wanted to avoid future plane crashes. Although this was the first plane crash since the incidence of the flood, lives had been lost together with goods worth thousands of dollars. The government couldn't risk another plane crash anymore. Families who had lost their loved ones during the crash were compensated and the damaged parts of the park were undergoing construction and repairs. The Ministry of Aviation Affairs stated that drones would be used instead of the planes to fly in supplies and to harvest fish from the nearby water around the city. I had seen drones in pictures, on the internet, and on the TV. But I was particularly thrilled that I was going to see them fly overhead pretty soon.

The following Saturday, I invited Cassy, Andrew, and Dannie over for tea, so that we could go check out the Bryans' greenhouse. I have been frequenting their greenhouse once in a while and it had grown into a stunning place, especially when the rays of the sunlit the whole room and cast a glance on the plants. I couldn't wait to show the buddies. Mrs. Bryan already told me it was fine by her and her husband to bring the buddies over. So, Saturday was the day, and I was getting ready to go. It was Cassy who arrived first and I went to get the door, with Kula right behind me, jumping excitedly and stretching to open the door as well. Right after Cassy entered, the boys arrived, and we set to go over to Bryan's after drinking iced tea.

We met a couple of customers who had come to buy freshly cut vegetables from Mrs. Bryan. Just as she had planned, their greenhouse was supplying vegetables to groceries and the neighborhood as well. Mrs. Bryan had just finished selling off some fresh daffodils in a vase to an elderly lady when she sighted us and waved. As usual, she had her hat on and that warm smile of hers all over her face.

"There they are. Oh, come on in. Good to see some youngsters again" Mrs. Bryan said.

We all speak in unison "hello Mrs. Bryan" with each of us planting a kiss on her wrinkled cheeks. I introduced the buddies to her, and she smiled at each one of them, motioning us into the house with the wave of her hand.

"I love her smile," Cassy whispered to my ears giggling.

"I know right," Was the warm reply I gave Cassy.

A cold glass of lemonade ran down our throats with joy while we sat with Mrs. Bryan. Dannie requested another glass and Mrs. Bryan was delighted to fill another glass for him. Of course, we all weren't surprised. Dannie could even finish the whole jug that was served. He seemed to be always famished. When we were done, we were ushered to the greenhouse through the back door and Mr. Bryan was in the house. He seemed like he was waiting on us the whole time. He immediately began to show us around once we exchanged pleasantries. There were different compartments of greens, fruits, and flowers. I sniffed one of the Rose flowers, the Red Rose, and its fragrance funnily tickled my nose until I gave a loud sneeze. Mrs. Bryan thought I was allergic to the flower, but I told her it's been a while I inhaled a flower. I loved flowers and Mrs. Bryan said I could pluck some into a vase if I wanted to. I was happy too because mom always loved to have fresh flowers in the vase, sitting right at the center of her dining table.

Dannie kept on asking loads and loads of questions and Mr. Bryan seemed to enjoy the curiosity of the young boy. Some questions got him laughing so hard too. Andrew was out inspecting the broccolis, cucumbers, cabbage, carrots, and other salad mixes. Cassy clung to Mrs. Bryan, following her everywhere around the house and helping her whenever she wanted to reach for a plant or flower. We were also shown the pipes that watered the greenhouse, although Mr. Bryan said they had connected it underground to get water from the outskirts of the city that still had flood water. The plants were healthy, devoid of diseases, and pests. We took pictures of the greenhouse to show it off to other students at school.

"You remind me of my grandmother, Mrs. Bryan. She loved gardening too and had green hands." Cassy said while holding Mrs. Bryan's hand as we all walked back to the main house.

" Oh, do I? Thank you, Cassy. What happened to your grandma though? "

"She died during one of the turbulent floods in her city. I couldn't get to see her. I miss her though."

"Oh, dear. Sorry about that." Mrs. Bryan replied while she hugged Cassy.

We thanked Bryan's again while we were set to go and Dannie told Mr. Bryan that he would love to come around again, because of the greenhouse and the lemonades too. We all laughed and took another glass of lemonade before leaving. I plucked fresh roses to take home and dropped them in a flower vase. While we were about to leave, a car drove in and parked in front of the house. When its driver got down, I recognized him to be the same man I met when the greenhouse was undergoing construction. He was the man that had the same nose as Mr. Bryan. Mrs. Bryan introduced him to us as her first son. He shook hands with us and smiled in my direction, giving my hand a gentle squeeze. My instincts told me that he recognized me as well.

Chapter Seven

Mr. Joe Bryan as he was introduced by Mrs. Bryan was all dressed in a flight suit when we saw him. I already concluded that he was a military pilot because he was sturdy. His wedding band glittered under the sun's rays when he shook hands with us earlier. He was wearing an overall blue and that prompted the curiosity in Dannie again. We were all tired and about to go home, but Dannie wasn't leaving until all his questions got answered. That was how determined he was, and no one could stop him. When Cassy, Andrew, and I realized what was happening, we decided to wait a bit just so we could all leave together. After all, it wouldn't hurt to learn a thing or two about the military from Mr. Joe Bryan. Mrs. Bryan already left for the house when she realized we wanted to have a chat with her son.

"Mr. Joe, why are you wearing a flight suit? Are you a pilot?" Dannie asked with his hands stroking his red hair.

"Well, I am a civilian drone pilot. I fly drones, commercial drones around different cities and states. I just got back from my last trip and I came over to see my folks."

"Oh! That is so cool." Dannie yelled and ran over to the side of Mr. Joe. Cassy, Andrew, and I also had excitement written all over our faces. The excitement seemed to have formed creases on our foreheads. I became more relaxed and I wanted to hear every detail that Mr. Joe had to share. We all knew that Drones were going to take over planes any moment from now as the government had stated. That alone got all of us listening with wide eyes to hear all that Mr. Joe had to say.

"So, Mr. Joe, do you wear a protective layer under a flight suit?" Cassy asked with her hands on the rim of her glasses.

He chuckled before replying, "you guys are a bunch of curious kids and I love intellectual kids. I'll tell you." He then began to demonstrate by opening a few buttons of his suit to show us what was being worn under a flight suit.

"Yeah guys, there's a special scarf that is being worn and tucked under the flight suit. It serves to conceal any undershirt worn under the flight suit." He then showed us the scarf under his suit, it was white.

"Then we also wear some customized gloves too. Sage green Nomex flight gloves with the AF-style green flight suits. So, we wear either sage green, dark blue, or black NOMEX flight gloves with the CAP blue flight suit. I know y'all not familiar with these terms, but you could always look it up on the internet." Mr. Joe Bryan said.

"Are you going to harvest fish with the drones too, Mr. Joe?" Andrew asked itching his eyes. He seemed sleepy.

"Yes. It's part of what the government would have us do at this time. Since airplanes aren't gonna be active anymore, we drone pilots are going to be extra busy now." Mr. Joe explained in between a yawn.

When he was done speaking, tiredness was written all over his face and we were also wary of standing that long.

"Well, it was nice meeting you buddies, Dannie especially. He seemed to have a lot of questions sitting in his pocket." He laughed before he went on,

"Well-done guys. But I gotta get inside now. Got to catch some rest before my next trip." Mr. Joe said.

We thanked him for his time and shook hands once more with him. We all needed to get going too. When Mr. Joe had disappeared into the house, the buddies and I were already on the road, strolling back to our houses. I hugged Cassy and shook hands with Dannie and Andrew before moving ahead while the other buddies went the other direction. I was spent but satisfied with all the info that Mr. Joe had delivered to us. I skipped a few times then started jogging down the street, eager to get home before dinner time.

I scribbled down all that Mr. Joe had told us about and I was elated that I had a drone pilot as a friend. At least I was sure that I was going to get to see a drone pretty soon, with Mr. Joe and the buddies. That night, I fell asleep almost immediately after my head hit my bed. My eyes fluttered open at exactly six in the morning. For the first time, I slept peacefully without a hint of a nightmare in my sleep. When I got to school that day, Dannie's voice was the first to greet me at school. He seemed hyperactive that morning.

"Hi, Katy. What's up? I guess you slept pretty hard last night. Your eyes seem to have doubled in size within the last ten hours." He chuckled.

"Yeah, Dannie. I actually did have a good sleep last night. What's up? Why are you all jumpy and all?"

"I looked up the terms that Mr. Joe Bryan had told us about and I learned a lot. I think I'd want to become a Drone pilot when I am grown, Katy," he replied smiling. Dannie was just too curious and funny at the same time. He seemed to switch over to the two traits simultaneously. I walked down the hall with him when the first bell was rung.

"So, Dannie, would you share what you looked up on Google with us?" I asked while the buddies and I were eating during the lunch hour.

"Sure. Nomex is a heat and flame meta-aramid fiber used across a diverse range of applications. It is used as a key component in fabrics utilized to create protective apparel. I guess that's one of the reasons the drone pilots wear it on as a form of gloves and shoes." Dannie said.

We went on conversing when without warning, we heard a strident sound, as though it was directly atop the roof of the cafeteria. We all ran out in our numbers to catch a glimpse of what the noise was about. There it was flying overhead, a drone! It looked more like a gigantic bird than an aircraft. Students were screaming and hopping loud with excitement at the sight of the drone. DACK were also screaming, with Dannie smiling all over the place as if he had just won a million-dollar lottery.

"Maybe Mr. Joe Bryan is the pilot," Andrew said when the drone was out of sight. We were ushered back inside by our teachers when calmness had returned back to the school premises.

Drones had begun to hover over houses and residential areas ever since the government had given the order. The US Army had also begun to assist the general public with the use of drone technology. The commercial drones had special fishing nets installed in them to capture fishes on sight and make the fishing way easier. Though the military drones were used strictly for security purposes around state boundaries, the US Army also invented special drones that would be able to detect large underwater activities of fish even from a longer distance.

Fishing activities had resumed with the drones fishing and harvesting large fishes from the seas. The flooded areas around the glassed cities were said to be reducing bit by bit according to the news headlines. Although sea levels were still threatening to rise, hence the outskirts of the cities were still very much in danger. All thanks to the glasshouses surrounding various cities and states. At least an air of safety was still hanging around.

One of the things that Mr. Joe Bryan had talked about that Saturday evening was how the drones were being able to harvest fish competently and accurately. He said that the drones would first scout the potential areas for fishing while flying 30 feet above the seawater so that the fishes do not detect the noise from the propeller of the drone. The drones could also spot potential areas where fish may gather. Provided the water is clear enough, the drone can see to a good depth of about 400 feet beneath its sonars. When curiosity took a grip on me, I further dived into various websites to learn more about drones and fishing.

Mom and I went over to the grocery store to grab some groceries. When we were done picking up various items, we went over to the grocer. Just when mom was about to pay, a group of men walked into the store, carrying fishes in crates amongst other essentials. The drones were also bringing in essentials from other places and supplying to various groceries across town. I walked over to see the fishes brought in and they were cool. Some had bloodstains all over while others were still wiggling. It was obvious they had just been caught. Mom came over to my side to see what had captured my attention so strongly. The grocer then said that those were the fishes harvested by the drones and that they were going to undergo processing shortly. I was super happy and excited to see the fishes for reasons I couldn't explain.

There was just a bumbling warmth of emotions rising on my inside. All through the drive home, my mind wondered at the way things had taken a turn in the last few years. The flood had come without any warning and brought with it a wave of change in towns, states, and even the various countries around the world. Sturdy glass walls were guarding the cities against the flood, greenhouses were now everywhere, serving as a major alternative for farming and now Drones had become a part of our society. Flying overhead, harvesting fishes, and bringing in supplies, the Drones had come to stay. We aren't going to remain the same again even if the flood dried out. We just can't be the same again, I muttered to myself as mom brought the car to a halt on the driveway.

The STF scheme organized yet another meeting of their volunteers and workers. Ever since school resumed fully, we the school kids rescheduled our meetings to the weekends. Some other volunteers who weren't high school kids held normal meetings during weekdays and we were briefed on weekends. I was tying my shoelaces, ready to go for the meeting when mom called me downstairs.

"Katy, come see what's on the news. You need to see this, hurry!"

"Okay, mom. Coming now " I hurried down the stairs smiling. Ever since we heard about the installation of greenhouses around the city, mom had become accustomed to the news. She wasn't as committed to the news as dad and me, but that unconcerned attitude of hers towards the news had taken a bow. When I got to the sitting room, there it was on the news: "Drones to be used for farming and construction." Recent research had it that drones could also be controlled to break the soil, dig deep ridges, and turn over the soil. This would serve as a way of improving and restoring the soil's fertility. Drones would be used for mechanized farming and normal planting of seeds could return. Before the drones would start digging up the soil, it would have detected areas that are still clogged, or close to being clogged by the sensors installed on the drone. Only trained drone pilots would be allowed to carry out these agricultural assignments on the large-scale, while smaller drones that could be owned by individuals who could afford them, would be licensed and permitted to practice small-scale farming. There would be schedules for the number of drones that would be allowed to operate at a time, to control the number of drones flying in a given city at a time to minimize the risk of crashes.

Mom and I finished listening to the news and mom had a bright smile lit on her face.

"Why are you smiling mom?"

"Well, I am just amazed at the way things are turning out. I'm also happy that normal farming activities can return to a large extent. Greenhouses plus normal farming activities, that means there would be lots of food for every one baby!" Mom exclaimed. She loved cooking and trying out new recipes. But the floods and scarcity of foods earlier, prevented and reduced her culinary exploits. Now that food was on the rise, I knew mom was going to explore every bit of her cookbook again.

I was so carried away that I didn't even know when time trailed past my STF meeting scheduled, and my ears were so occupied, they didn't hear the sound of my phone beeping upstairs. I ran upstairs to pick my phone and five missed calls; two from Cassy, one from Dannie and Andrew each, and the other from the STF coordinator were all staring right back at me in the face. I was twenty minutes late for the meeting. I picked my bag and hurried out of the house, with the wind whipping strands of my hair wildly all over the place as I biked to the meeting venue. When I arrived, they were halfway gone into the meeting. I slipped through quietly and sat behind Cassy while the head of the volunteering team went on talking.

"Why are you late? " Cassy whispered.

"Well, I was lost in the news update," I replied whispering back.

The STF coordinator had stated that we would be visiting the glasshouse for the homeless to supply them with essentials and to check upon them. It was part of the schedule of the STF scheme as the government had ordered, to ensure that they were faring well. I was very elated because I knew I was going to see little Tina again. The very thought of seeing her smile warmed my heart ahead.

The glasshouse smelt the same and the population didn't seem tampered with at all. Same old smell of people, normal people that had one issue or the other, trying to survive like everyone else in the world. I kept on scouting around for Tina. When it didn't look like she was going to show up anytime soon, I kept on with my duties with other volunteers. My eyes finally caught a glimpse of Tina, but there was a cold air hanging around her. Her eyes seemed to have grown cold and wild when they locked with mine. We were a few meters away from each other, but Tina's tiny feet seemed glued to the ground. She just kept on throwing cold stares at me.

Eventually, I began moving towards her. When I held her hands, she didn't budge until she was wrapped in my embrace. I expected her mom to come out and see me or take Tina with her, as was her normal custom whenever Tina and I met but Tina's mom was nowhere to be seen. I knew something was amiss, but my instincts couldn't place what it was exactly.

I was still standing with Tina's hand in mine when one of the female coordinators of the glasshouse approached. She was a young woman in her mid-thirties, and she had the expression of a turbulent sea that had just witnessed calmness.

"Hello miss. I see you are one of the STF workers."

"Well, I'm a volunteer actually. Katy's the name." I replied with my hands stretched to hers.

"My name is Grace, and I am the coordinator of the homeless children's compartment." She said with my hands in hers.

"Oh, that's a good one. The last time we came visiting, there were no children compartment coordinators. Each child was under the care of a parent, right?"

"Yeah, you are absolutely right. But we had to set up that special compartment amongst other existing ones to cater to children like Tina who have no parents to fend for them."

"Hold on a second, hold on. The last time I checked Tina had a mom, and she was always on the lookout for Tina. What are you saying?" I exclaimed with the pitch of my voice startling Tina. The little girl just clutched onto me tightly.

"Well, yes you are right, but Tina lost her mom to cancer just a week ago. She..."

" No, this can't be happening. No! " I cut in with tears racing down my cheeks.

Now everything was beginning to make perfect sense. This was probably the reason why I felt an earlier pang of uneasiness in my heart. No wonder Tina wasn't her usual self that day.

I began to cry so loudly, Cassy heard my voice and came over to my side, asking questions that my voice wouldn't permit me to answer. My soul had fallen silent just like Tina's. I held the little girl to my chest, stroking her gently while my tears soaked her dress.

Tina was too little to understand what death was, but I knew that a part of her was feeling empty and lonely. Tina held on to me the rest of that evening and she began to cry profusely when it was time for us to leave.

All through the drive back home in the STF bus, I couldn't say a word. My voice seemed to have been buried beneath a heap of sorrows and grief. Other STF workers and volunteers couldn't help but throw concerned stares at me all the while, but I didn't budge. Miss Grace had told Cassy about Tina's mom and Cassy had stood by my side ever since, patting my back gently from time to time. A part of me seemed to have died the moment I got to know about Tina's mom's death. I didn't even know her name.

"Why wasn't I able to see cancer in her eyes? Why didn't I see that she was dying by the minute, Why? Why?" I sobbed loudly into mom's arms. Mom had noticed my fallen expression when I got back from the STF outreach and she immediately knew something was wrong. I broke into tears when she reached out to me and cried to my heart's content before finally telling her what had happened to Tina's mom. I could see tears well up in mom's eyes.

That night, I saw Tina's mom in my dream. She looked much healthier and her eyes had those hazel hues that enveloped me with warmth all over again. She was calling out to me and saying words that I couldn't comprehend. She was calling out of a hollow sphere, but my hands couldn't reach out to her.

When I woke up the next morning, I had puffy eyes staring back at me in the mirror and my head continued to throb. I couldn't eat most of that day and I stayed back at home from school. I realized that morning that death wasn't just the opposite of life. Death was a part of life and it could come knocking at anyone's door, anytime it wanted. Our end game is death.

Chapter Eight

"Copper-colored liquid? No, brown colored water, or do I call it muddy water?" I muttered to myself when I turned the kitchen faucet. A thousand different colors were mixing in my head and turning upside down as I stared at the water. I couldn't believe what I was seeing. The faucet was leaking what was supposed to be water, but what it leaked looked like some sandy water, almost the color of tea. Mom and dad had stepped out for a walk, so there was no one to see the same thing I was seeing. Kula was by my legs, wagging and panting, her red tongue sticking out like she wanted to see the colored water too.

"What could be happening again?" I yelled aloud, waiting for a reply but all I could hear was my echo, resounding all over the kitchen. Ever since I was a little girl, I had never seen dirty water oozing out of the faucets in the house. Water came through underground pipes and was distributed to various homes around the city. Even when the ground was clogged, it didn't stop clean water from rushing through the taps. I assumed that it was the kitchen faucet that was faulty, so I raced upstairs and went to my bathroom to turn on the faucet. It was the same copper-colored water that seeped out from the tap and even the shower. Mom had complained during dinner at the table the previous night, that the water was a bit murky when she was about to start cooking. Well, since she was going to boil some of the water, I didn't really care but now that the water was like a puddle, I had a thousand and one reasons to care.

Mom and dad weren't back yet so I decided to ring Cassy, just so I'd know if she had the same water issues too,

"Hey, girl! What's up?"

"Katy I'm not okay at all! I'm just about to take a shower and the water looks like mud. I don't know what's going on girl. Maybe our pipes are rusty or something?"

"Wow! That's why I called you. The water leaking from the faucets in my house is also colored and dense... Something must be wrong. I just hope it's not what I'm thinking Cassy."

"Are you thinking underground water has been polluted?"

"Exactly! I think that maybe the flood water or even the seawater has seeped through the groundwater and messed it all up. We have another problem on our hands, Cassy."

"Yeah. But just like always, I'm sure the agencies would look into it. I gotta go now, Katy. I gotta go find some 'clean' water to shower. Bye girl"

"Bye, Cassy." I hung up, wondering where Cassy was going to get clean water at this time. I began to recollect what clean water looked like. The liquid leaking out of the faucet seemed to have stolen the picture of what crystal-clear water looked like, from my memory.

Dannie and Andrew gave the same reports about the water systems in their houses and that was when I concluded my hypothesis that the city's water supply had been contaminated. I knew that sooner or later the news headlines would have it that there had been contamination of water around. I couldn't tell if other cities had the same issues too, I could only wait to hear what the news had to say.

I didn't even wait for mom and dad's return when I clicked on the news channel. My theory was right, the government and the US Water Corporation body had declared a state of emergency. The news correspondent had reported that research has it that the flood water had seeped through the groundwater and contaminated it. The contamination might have occurred through broken, underground pipes. It was advised that no one drink the water, as it could pose a high risk of diseases if consumed. In the meantime, the government was going to deliver bottled water to homes until there was a way out. I couldn't imagine how many bottles of water could satisfy the thirst of the entire population. Water couldn't be compared to food that could be easily distributed to satisfy immediate wants. Water was needed for other domestic and sanitary activities around the house.

"There has to be another way out," I muttered to myself while waiting for mom and dad to return.

Water scarcity was the talk of the school. Students were chatting and conversing about the color of the water, what the news had reported, and how we were going to survive. The buddies and I also got talking during the break.

"We got a huge problem on our hands, guys, and this one seems like the worst one ever. I drink water a lot and now I have to minimize the number of bottles in a day? hell! " Dannie said while wiping beads of sweat off his face.

"Well, I had to even boil the water, let it settle for some ten minutes, and filtered it before taking a shower this morning," I explained.

"Hold on, Katy! Did you just say you boiled and filtered the water before bathing?" Andrew asked with a small smile across his face.

"Yeah, I did, and the color was almost crystal clear after I did so."

"Cool! That's a great idea. I'm gonna try it out when I get home. You wouldn't believe I showered with six bottles of water this morning. It's my little secret though." Andrew replied laughing.

Cassy and Dannie also welcomed the idea and said that they were going to do the same when they got home. I had read about how contaminated water could be treated and one of the ways mentioned was boiling and filtering. Even though the water from the faucet looked like it wasn't going to get rid of its copper coat, it became almost as good as crystal when I finished filtering and I felt really proud of myself. It wasn't safe for drinking though.

It wasn't even a week yet and the news update read that several lives had been lost due to the consumption of contaminated water. Viral infections seemed to be on the rise, and it was taking lives by the minute. Even hospitals and health workers began to cry out that hospital beds were filling up and they didn't have anywhere else to keep patients. Some of my classmates had also fallen ill too as the attendance of students decreased by the day. The government seemed overwhelmed and had officially announced that every city should find out its own means of survival from this water crisis. They promised to support any solution that could suffice. Ever since the day the government had announced that bottled water would be distributed to homes, I knew that they had run out of ideas because the population was too large for bottled water to satisfy.

The next STF volunteer meeting came up and I looked forward to it with so much enthusiasm because DACK had come up with plans on simple ways to make polluted water drinkable again. When Dannie, Cassy, and Andrew tried out my method of boiling and filtering, they realized that it had reduced the density of the water to a minimal level and saw that the water was almost as good as crystal clear.

Since then, we all tasked ourselves individually to look up ways that contaminated water could be made clean again on the Internet. We promised each other that we were going to read voraciously on the topic and share our ideas during the next STF volunteer meeting. Now the day had come, and I couldn't wait to hear what the buddies had found out.

Dannie was the first to speak up when the STF coordinator asked if anyone had opinions and ideas to share about ways, we could tackle the issue on the ground.

"I came across a water filter straw online that could be used to make contaminated water drinkable again. The straw could filter about 4000 liters of water, enough for one person for three years! See, that could last us the whole-time guys. It could also remove almost all waterborne diseases, bacteria, and parasites. The best part about this straw is that it can filter and provide clean water without the use of chemicals and batteries." Dannie explained.

Some of the volunteers and workers were already applauding Dannie even before he was done speaking.

"Wow, wow, wow! That's a brilliant find, Dannie. Great job buddy, great job. Anyone got questions or suggestions to Dannie's idea?" The STF coordinator asked."

"I have a question, Dannie. First off, that's a brilliant concept you got there but what would be the material used to manufacture these water filter straws?" The freckled blonde lady asked Dannie. She was the assistant coordinator of the STF team.

"They are made from hollow fiber membrane and they also incorporate an activated carbon component," Dannie replied.

Andrew also brought up the idea of adding chlorine and iodine into cloudy or colored water to disinfect the water and make it suitable for use.

"Woah! I never knew iodine could filter water too!" The STF coordinator exclaimed.

"Well, you could use a few tinctures of iodine added to a liter of water to disinfect it. If the water is very colored, 10 drops of iodine would do. Then it would be left to stand for at least thirty minutes before use." Andrew slowly explained.

Cassy also shared her idea of using alum to help suspended particles settle down. She also stated that the process of decantation and filtering would also help. I also mentioned the fact that boiling and filtering the water with filter cartridges and filter bowls would make the water safe. A young man in our midst also mentioned that passing the water through layers of large sand beds helps in the filtration as well.

When the suggestions and questions had calmed, the STF coordinator said that we were going to organize campaigns to enlighten the public about these ways of water purification. He also stated that since we were working with the government, they would provide some of the materials like chlorine, filter clothes, decantation containers, sand beds, and other equipment that would be distributed freely to homes to make their waters drinkable.

One of the cities in Connecticut began to find a way around their water issue. They collected large liters of flood and seawater from the outskirts of their environs, stored them in large reservoirs, filtered it with chlorine and other chemicals, then distributed it through above-ground pipes to homes and the city at large. That was their way of reducing the amount of floodwater around their vicinity. Some other cities used solar energy to power large machines that would filter reservoirs of water through the reverse osmosis method and distribute it around. The news had stated that each city was beginning to be self-sufficient by the day.

STF campaigns already started in our city and we began to inform the public about ways to make polluted water drinkable again. I was super excited to be part of the campaign, alongside Cassy, Dannie, and Andrew. The water filter straws were approved promptly by the U.S. Food and Drug Administration Agency (FDA) and were manufactured by a plastics company that distributed them to people. During the campaign, Dannie displayed how the water filter straw could be used; a bowl of colored water was placed in front of him. Next, he inserted the water filter straw into the colored water. By the time he sucked the water into the straw, it was as good as clean without any particles. Everyone was thrilled when he was done. That day, I wore joy like a second skin, because I was directly part of those that provided life solutions to the water scarcity in the city. It was a dream come true for me and the rest of the buddies.

"Hello, Katy."

"Hello, Andrew. What's up? Your voice sounds low. Any problem?"

"Katy, my mom's down with the fever and it's really bad."

"I'm so sorry about your mom Andrew, but she'd pull through okay?"

"Yeah. I hope she does"

"What hospital is she in? I could tell my mom so we can stop by sometime."

"She's in New Haven's Hospital. Whenever you wanna come around, just let me know so that I'd wait for you guys in the front lobby of the hospital."

"Alright, Andrew. Stay strong and your mom will definitely pull through. Bye, Andrew."

When I clicked off the phone, I could only hope that Andrew's mother would pull through. It has been months since I heard the news of Tina's mom's demise and I still felt the emptiness in my soul. Now that Andrew's mom was ill, I hoped that she wouldn't disappear with death, Andrew wouldn't be able to handle it. I whispered a prayer under my breath as I walked down the stairs to tell mom about Andrew's mother.

Chapter Nine

The sun didn't shine that day. It was like every other day. No birds were tweeting, the clouds seemed pregnant with rain and I could hear the whistle of the breeze tapping against my window. It was just a normal, cool morning when Andrew texted me that his mother had bit the dust. It was a very brief text, one that sent daggers into my heart as soon as my eyes locked with the line,

"The fever took my mom."

Tears trickled down my cheeks as the rain trickled outside my window. I scanned through my memory to recollect what Andrew's mom looked like. I could see a picture of her smiling faintly at me and mom, the last time we checked up on her at the hospital. Andrew was waiting outside by the hospital's driveway when mom's car pulled in. I hugged him and mom gave his shoulder a gentle squeeze before ushering us to the ICU where his mother lay. We couldn't go in, but we could see through the huge, glass pane standing between us and Andrew's mom. I knew her to be a plump woman with beautiful eyes dancing within their sockets. Her eyes reminded me of a thousand blue seas. But now that I beheld her, she had been reduced to a small physique and her skin seemed to have glued with her bones. Even her eyes seemed to have lost their blue hue.

"I am so sorry Andrew," I whispered into his ears, holding his hands while tears raced down my face. Mom wasn't left out either, she just kept on dabbing her eyes the whole time we were at the hospital. A few days ago, when I visited Andrew's mom, she gave a faint smile when her eyes fluttered open before we left the hospital. When I got home that day, I knew it would take a miracle to save Andrew's mom from the grip of the fever. It had eaten deep into her body, way too much. I was hoping for a miracle, but it did not transpire.

The thunderbolt reverberating on the roof blinked me back to the present and by the time I ran to look out of my window, I couldn't believe what I was seeing. Another flood was threatening, the water on the roads had risen and the rainfall was intense. It didn't look like it was going to calm anytime soon. I raced downstairs to see what the news had to say. I knew that I wasn't stepping a foot out of the house for the rest of this Saturday. All thanks to the downpour.

Mom and dad were already preoccupied with the news, they didn't even notice when I slipped past them and sat on the sofa. The breaking news had it that the sea levels were threatening to rise again and that any further rainfall might result in both external and internal flooding. I remembered that the glass walls were built tall around the city. If the rainwater continued at the same rate over a while, the sea levels may rise above that and flood the entire city like never before. The government however advised that water be pumped out of the cities. This would serve as a means of reducing the amount of water on the streets. Dad switched off the television while the news was still on.

"Why did you turn it off, honey? The news is still on." mom asked with a bewildered frown on her face. Dad replied that he was tired of the hurdles we had to live with and that we were all going to die if the city ever got flooded. I could detect panic in dad's voice while he spoke.

"Dad, don't worry we would be fine. Even if the city gets flooded, I'm sure there would be a way out okay?"

"Okay Sweetie, I do hope we would be fine. What's wrong with your eyes, Katy? Have you been crying? Common talk to me what's up? Dad asked, concern written all over his face. It was when dad spoke that mom came and sat beside me.

"Andrew's mom didn't make it. She died this morning." I replied gently, with tears threatening to drop from my eyes. Mom stroked my hair and buried my head on her chest, patting my back lightly while I sobbed. She was also crying too. She had known Andrew's mom right from the time we were all in the glasshouse. They had seen each other a couple of times at school too. Mom told she knew that Andrew's mom might not make it, but she wanted to keep hope alive. Dad didn't know what to say, he just stood up, kissed us both on our foreheads, and went upstairs. The rest of the day went on quietly, with the rain reduced to drizzles towards the evening. Even the weather seemed to be mourning the death of a soul.

After two days, the waters had subsided to a drastic degree. The ground was still wet and a bit slippery, but not as clogged as it was the first time it rained this intensely. People could move freely without fear of getting stuck in the mud or drenched with rain. I took a walk down the path to clear my head. Andrew's mom's death had been on my mind for a day and I couldn't tell what was going to happen to Andrew. He had told me earlier one sunny afternoon at school that his parents were divorced, and his older brother was far away studying at a college. His dad was as good as dead to him because his parents got separated even before Andrew turned one. Now that his mom was gone, I knew it was going to take a toll on the overall wellbeing of Andrew. I liked him and I didn't want to see him in misery. A thousand and one different thoughts raced across my mind while I strolled down the street, with my hands buried in my pocket.

"Hi, Katy. Katy! Katy!! Katy!!!" Mr. Joe Bryan yelled from the window of his car. I didn't even notice that his car had halted right by me.

"Hello, Mr. Bryan," I replied with a half-smile.

" Hi Katy, you seem lost in thought. You didn't even hear my voice and you don't even have earphones on. Wanna talk?"

I opened the car and hopped into the passenger seat, hugging my jacket close. The weather seemed to have changed into a colder coat. I rubbed my palms together, blowing air into them at intervals while Mr. Bryan drove on. I didn't know where he was headed, but I needed to clear my head. I told Mr. Bryan about Andrew's mom and even though he never knew what she looked like; I could see a concerned look on his face.

"I am so sorry about that Katy. Heard from your friend yet? How's he holding up?"

"Well, the last time I spoke with him, his voice seemed lost and I knew he had been crying. Cassy, Dannie, and I did visit him, but he could only nod and turn his head sideways while we conversed with him. He didn't say a word and his face was down most of the time. His aunt was with him."

"I am so sorry about that." Mr. Bryan said again. I told him it was fine but I received two deaths within a short time, which were beginning to affect me. I told him about Tina and her mom and how hard it was for me to leave Tina all alone, the last time I visited the glasshouse.

"How old is the little girl?"

"You mean Tina?"

"Yeah."

"Well, she has recently turned three. But you would never believe it when you saw her because she has the eyes of a ten-year-old." I explained to Mr. Bryan with a chuckle.

"That's interesting." He replied nodding his head and tapping his index finger on his chin while driving. He seemed lost in thought.

Mr. Bryan was heading to the grocery store. He stepped down to get some groceries while I stayed back in the car to enjoy the heater in the car. Outside seemed too cold for my body. I calmed myself a bit and my thoughts seemed to be packed in one piece after taking a cruise with Mr. Bryan. Maybe I just needed a change of environment. Mr. Bryan returned to the car a few minutes later with bags of groceries and a Snickers bar for me. I munched on while we headed back home.

"So, how's fishing so far, Mr. Bryan? I heard on the news that the sea levels had risen and were threatening to keep rising. Is that true?" I asked Mr. Bryan with my mouth full of the last piece of the Snicker bar.

"Yes, Katy. It is true. The waters have risen faster than we imagined in the last couple of weeks. We've even had to stop fishing for a while because we couldn't fly close to the water. It would be too dangerous. That's part of the reason I'm around and not on duty, flying the fishing Drone." He explained.

"Oh, I see. Do you think the water could outweigh the glass walls built around the city?"

"Well, yes Katy. If the water continues to rise steadily, it will get over the glass walls and the entire city could be flooded. It's actually an emergency that calls for immediate action, but the government seems relaxed."

When Mr. Bryan dropped me in front of my house, I thanked him for the ride and waved till his car was out of sight, but I couldn't stop thinking about the last statement he made,

"The rising sea levels is an emergency that calls for immediate action."

That night, I dreamt that water had taken over the entire city and I saw myself buried within the grip of the ocean again. I was struggling to breathe through my lungs, but my entire body felt bloated. The dream was still vivid, when I woke up, sweating and shivering.

Andrew's mom was laid to rest and he cried all through the burial procession. I held his hands all through the burial, trying to calm him down. Dannie and Cassy also stood close, patting him on his back alternately during the burial. Some of our classmates and teachers were present too. I knew that something in Andrew had died the same day his mom died. I just hoped that he wasn't going to slip into depression in the days to come.

The research was going on, as ways to secure the entire city from being flooded, as the seawater wasn't going down at all. Some scientists had taken the tour of the rising sea levels with a drone and predicted that within the next few months to come, the entire state would be flooded. Their reports had prompted the government to start acting and once again all hands were on the deck.

Neighboring cities were also on the lookout for ways to prevent the impending flood. The waters had come to stay, but we had to find a permanent means of survival. I continued to read up from different sources on the web. There just had to be a way out.

Andrew didn't show up at school for a week and his absence was being felt by me and the buddies.

"Andrew has not been in school for a week now. I really miss him you know." Dannie replied while we walked home.

"Well, I think he's really going through a lot. Maybe we could stop over at his house to check up on him." I replied.

Cassy had been on her phone ever since we were at the cafeteria, all through classes, and even now while we were on our way home. She seemed so absorbed in her phone. She didn't even hear me and Dannie conversing. I was about to tap her shoulders when she suddenly exclaimed,

"Oh my gosh! you wouldn't believe it guys. There's finally a way out. Turns out that the government has a plan B that would save us from the impending flood." she replied jumping while her left hand adjusted her glasses from falling off her face. I scurried close to her to see what the news had to say. My phone's battery was down so I couldn't get any notifications. Dannie just turned on his phone to see what Cassy was thrilled about.

"The US government has unveiled a plan B structure that would serve as a permanent solution in securing various cities from the flood. The structure would be built exactly like the desert dome in Nebraska. It would be able to accommodate a population ten times the size of the city's actual average population." I read out aloud from Cassy's phone with a huge smile spread across my lips.

"They plan to call the Nebraska-dome kind of structures, pods. And it would consist of a huge air circulator/purifier on the top to maintain the pressure inside the pod while allowing light into the pod. This sounds super cool guys!" Dannie yelled.

" I know Right! The whole pod idea has really made my evening. I guess we should tell Andrew while we stop by at his house. Maybe this news would lighten his mood." Cassy said.

The news did lighten Andrew's mood, at least he smiled when he came downstairs and met us all in his living room. He seemed to be lost inside the sweatshirt he had on and his eyes had bags sitting under them. But he still looked somewhat cute to me.

"Hey buddies, I'm thrilled to see y'all at my house today. "Andrew replied while he gave each of us a brief handshake before taking a seat by my side.

"How are you, buddy? I've really missed you on our team you know. You complete DACK, without Andrew, we'd just be DCK and that sounds so boring." Cassy replied smiling while she kept her hands busy wiping the lens of her glasses.

"I am sure no one misses you as much as I do. Now I'm the only guy stuck in between two girls with no Andrew to discuss football with. I miss you, Andrew. " Dannie replied giving Andrew a big high five while we all giggled. It was nice to see that Andrew was getting over his loss, gradually.

"I actually miss you guys too. I miss all the fun plus I know that I have loads of schoolwork piled up for me, but Mrs. Helen already said she would take me personal tutorials to catch up with the entire class whenever I am in the right mind to resume." Andrew replied gently.

"I've been upstairs all day. It was my aunt that informed me that you guys were around. I had to come to see you all. So, tell me, what's happening? I've been off any news update and my phone is switched off most of the day. So, what's up?"

It was Dannie who replied to Andrew, telling him about the recent news of the rising sea levels and the high risk it posed on the city and the entire state as well. Cassy then went on to tell him about the pod structure and the entire plan B that the government was about to commence.

Andrew smiled and asked questions that Dannie was so excited to provide answers to. I also informed him about Mr. Bryan's condolences. Andrew's aunt served us the glasses of cold lemonade and cookies. As always, Dannie was the first to empty his glass with his mouth full of cookies. We were already used to his ravenous appetite. We hugged Andrew warmly when it was time to leave and he assured us that he would be in school the following week. I was glad that the topic of his mom's death wasn't brought up at all. I knew he was still hurt inside but there seemed to be a bout of fresh air around him when we left his place. I could only hope that he would get better in the days to come.

Dad and mom were already aware of the plan B structure and the whole pod stuff. When I got home that evening, the news headlines already unveiled the proposed outline of the structure and it looked exactly like the desert dome in Nebraska. A transparent dome structure that has triangular panels interlocking with each other to create a strong dome that would help protect the city.

"So, dad, you realize there wasn't any need to panic? I told you there was going to be a way out. Let's just hope it works out perfectly."

"Well, I am sure it would. Thanks, Katy." Dad replied while I fell into his warm embrace.

Chapter Ten

It was Dannie who first complained about the transparent candy. We had all strolled to the grocery store after one of our STF volunteer meetings, to grab a snack. The STF coordinator had stated that the government had started research on the kind of material to be used to make the pod. They didn't want to use materials that would tear or fade out even when the floods came around. Intense research was presently ongoing in regard to the pod and the STF coordinator had told us to inform him about any plans or suggestions that either of us had towards the Plan B project. We had a short break in the middle of the meeting and Dannie indicated that we go grab some snacks at the grocery store close by.

The candy was transparent, more like a sweet glass in the shape of a ball. It was Dannie who complained about it first after popping the sweet into his mouth a few times,

"Damn! This candy is just too hard. I can't even get to chew it. It hurts really bad." Dannie said with his hands on his jaw, as if he had a toothache.

Cassy also tried to take a bite but gave a shrill cry when she tried to crush the candy in between her teeth. We had already paid for the candy, but we were still standing outside the store. So, I ran in to have a few words with the grocer. Holding two candies in my hand,

"Hello, sir. Well, I figured we might have a little problem on our hands."

The grocer had the face of a man who had been into a few wrestling matches, but his voice and physique were totally different from that of a wrestler. His voice sounded like a hummingbird by the time he gently replied. I was tempted to tell him that he had a sweet voice, but I didn't want to digress from the subject of the candy at hand.

"Well, young lady, I suppose the candy is a little too hard for you to chew right?"

"How did you know I was going to talk about candy?"

"You got two of them sticking out of your hands. I am sorry you had to pay for it, before realizing it was hard. I probably should take them off the candy shelf."

"Well, it's a little bit. too tough on the teeth, one might lose a whole dentition while trying to chew this you know. I bet you shouldn't have it displayed in the candy section anymore. It's really bad."

"I am so sorry you had to go through this. I got the candies delivered just this afternoon and you guys are the second customer that noticed its hardness. I haven't even tasted it myself. I'll take it off the shelves before other customers notice it. Thank you for your observation, Miss...."

"Katy's the name."

"Right. Please, you and your friends could keep the candies. I'd be glad to offer you guys other candies at no extra cost if you don't mind." the grocer replied. I called over the rest of the guys to come in to pick what they want in exchange. I still told him he had a sweet voice before I left the grocery store that day. It wasn't so bad to tell a kind word to a grocer.

When I got home that evening, I told mom about the candy and how I almost lost a molar trying to chew on the sweet. I showed mom the candy and she inspected it like it was some sacred glass stone while I put the other hard candy in my back pocket. I planned to keep it in my room for weeks to see if it would ever become soft if left for a long time under room temperature. Mom didn't even touch the candy, she just shoved it aside and told me to go brush my teeth while she went on with the dinner preparation.

I was already halfway up the stairs to my room when I heard the news correspondent mention something about a 'stone candy'.

"That must be the same candy they are talking about," I muttered to myself while running back down the stairs to watch the news. It was reported on the news that a special candy was in town and that there have been complaints about the hard texture of the candy. It was said on the news, that the manufacturer of the candy had stated that it was made from a particular kind of sugar cane, but it was just too hard to be chewed. The manufacturer claimed that he didn't intend to sell the candy off to the market and that further production of the candies had stopped, they were surprised to see the candy in some grocery stores.

"Maybe some of the workers had sent the candies out without the prior knowledge of the manufacturer. No one knows what exactly happened, but the government has placed a ban on the candy for now. They also closed the candy factory until further notice. More news to come, stay tuned to channel one. Yours Susan Matthews."

I was already on my way upstairs to take a shower when Cassy's call came in,

"Hey, girl! Did you watch the news?"

"Yeah, I just did. What about it?"

"Well, I noticed that it might have been a fake candy and you know we both had a taste of it. I've brushed nothing less than three times since I got home just in case the candy had a hint of poison in it."

"You really didn't have to do that Cassy. It's just a normal candy that didn't turn out well. I'm sure it's nothing" I replied in between bursts of laughter.

I continued laughing at what Cassy said even after I hung up the call. I knew that nothing was going to happen because we tasted the candy. Besides, the news said it was just too hard, they never mentioned that it had poison in them. I brought out the candy I had set aside in my back pocket and placed it on the table. I studied it for a few minutes before going to take a shower.

A Material Scientist and researcher had come across the candy and stated that it was the perfect material to be used to construct the pod. When interviewed on how he had come about his hypothesis, he explained that he bought some of the candies and set aside some of them in his workplace for further experiments. He then melted a large amount of the candy together and allowed it to cool.

"I noticed that the cooled mixture turned to be a very strong, lightweight transparent material. I added cubic silicon nitride to it, and I realized that it would be the strongest, transparent material ever. Thus, it would be very ideal in making the proposed pod."

"Why did you add silicon nitride to it?" Asked the female interviewer with inquisitive eyes.

"Cubic silicon nitride is transparent and stable up to 1400 degrees Celsius so I figured that this would make the material heat resistant and also increase its transparency and strength, making it an ideal material for the pod structure."

"Is the material waterproof too?" the inquisitive eyes asked the young researcher.

"Sure, it is. I threw some of the material into a fish glass tank and it did float. The amazing thing was water didn't get through it. It's a strong waterproof material. I suppose it is so because of the cane used to produce the candy. However, my fish tried to eat it while it was in the fish tank but I'm sure if it is coated with further chemicals like polyester, fishes wouldn't be able to get across to it. More so, research would still be ongoing."

The day that Andrew resumed back to school, was the same day that the government announced that they were going to start working on the huge Plan B project with the idea of the young researcher. Farmers had begun to grow the sugar cane in different greenhouses and regular farms. The entire populace had heard about the ongoing research. Since the sugar cane was the primary raw material, all hands were on the deck in ensuring that the sugar cane was available in a large quantity. Each city was going to construct its own dome with the help of the government. The pod would encompass the whole city and form a semi-spherical kind of covering around it, such that when the floods arrive, the pod would be left standing waterproof amid the floods.

Different see-through fabrics like Gossamer, silk, rayon, and nylon were being used in the construction of the pod to increase the transparency of the material. The pod was also going to undergo further waterproof spraying with polyurea, polycarbonate, and bituminous waterproofing. A self-healing material like polyester and elastomers were also going to be added to the materials used to coat the pod in certain sections. This would help to preserve the pod from wearing out or fading. The self-healing polymers would activate in response to an external stimulus like light, temperature change, and other factors to initiate the healing process. I was so thrilled with the information I was reading about the pod structure and the different components used to make the material. No doubt, it was a huge project that was going to cost millions of dollars, but it was worth every penny spent.

"Well, it turns out that the 'stone candy' happens to be our little hero," Dannie said while we were having lunch at the cafeteria and we all laughed about it. I had earlier told Andrew about the candy and he was as scared as Cassy. That day, Andrew had also told me to go brush my mouth too just in case the candy had some poison in it.

"No kidding! Cassy and Andrew, there was really nothing to be worried about. It was just some sort of sweet stone. It had no harmful substance in it." I explained to the buddies while we kept on laughing. We were glad to have Andrew back on the team again and even if he wasn't as cheerful as his usual self, he didn't seem to have gotten over his grief completely. I was sure pleased to see that he had gotten over the bags under his eyes completely. I figured that when we lose loved ones, we might never get over the grief, we seem to just live on with the grief locked up in some corner of our hearts. That was what Andrew had done. He had locked up his mom's grief in the quiet corner of his heart and I tried my best not to unlock that corner, anytime soon.

That night, my eyes lay awake to the silence that hung in the dark. I had turned off my reading lamp, but sleep seemed far away from me. All I could wrap my head around was the impending flood. I knew deep down within me that I was scared. The plan B project was going smoothly, and the government had even stated that the pod would be ready in no time. If the floods did come, everything would be drowned and swept under the ocean bed. What if the pod couldn't withstand the torrents of the flood? What if some huge fishes came out of the water and swallowed the whole pod? What if water was truly going to destroy us all? All these thoughts and more raced across my mind like lightning across the sky. When my eyes fluttered open the next morning, I was more than grateful that sleep found me after all.

The pod was beginning to take shape and had similar features as the geodesic desert dome in Nebraska. Mr. Stanford had displayed a projection on the whiteboard to show us what the Desert dome looked like and what the ongoing pod construction looked like. The pod was built in a spherical structure based on a network of beams arranged on great circles lying on the surface of a sphere. The geodesics intersect to form triangular elements that create local triangular rigidity and distribute the stress.

Curiosity had a better part of Dannie and he raised his hands to ask a question while Mr. Stanford was teaching. Even though Mr. Stanford was gruff and old, he still always tolerated Dannie's inquisitiveness.

"What's the meaning of geodesic?" Dannie asked.

"It means a lot of things my boy but in the context of the pod, it means the domed structure of lightweight straight elements forming interlocking polygons," replied Mr. Stanford.

Mr. Stanford was still my best teacher, because of my love for geography.

Chapter Eleven

"Imagine putting your hand through a jelly-like material to get hold of something. Imagine poking your hands through the pod to catch a fish swimming just in front of your eyes. Imagine..."

"Wait! Cut it out, Katy. I don't want to imagine anymore. Are you trying to say that we would be able to fish directly with our hands while in the pod? That sounds super creepy and scary girl!" Cassy exclaimed with goosebumps all over her arms while we sat down under the cool breeze of the park. DACK had decided to hang out on a picnic just to have fun and feel the breeze of the wind caress our faces.

"Well Cassy, it's high time we faced reality. The pod is almost ready, and the floods would come knocking anytime soon. Scientists already stated that the sea levels would continue to rise and the whole city would be flooded. It means while we are safe in the pod, the flood water would envelop us all. Remember it's a transparent glass, so you'd get to see lots of fishes swimming in front of your eyes. It sounds like it's going to be a whole lot of fun." Dannie replied with a sandwich in his hand.

"But guys, have you ever thought about the possibility of we being cut off from other cities if the pod is finished? Of course, I know every city had been surviving on its own for a couple of years now, but I think there should still be a means of communication with other 'pods' right?" Andrew asked calmly.

"Hmmm, that's a point you got there, Andrew. I've never really thought about it but there should actually be a means of communication between pods." I replied.

"I've been thinking of the homeless people at the glasshouse for a couple of days now, Katy. We only visit them when the STF volunteers and workers tell us to. We could go visit them as a team to show that we care for them. We might not even be able to go with anything, but our visitation would surely go a long way in their hearts. What do you think guys?" Cassy asked with her hands incessantly fiddling with her hair. Cassy always seemed to get her hands busy whenever she was talking. I was glad that she wasn't cleaning her lens as always.

We all agreed to Cassy's idea and decided that we would pay a visit to the glasshouse. My mind drifted to Tina. I wondered if she was faring well even with the absence of her mom.

"That's a great idea you got there Cassy. I'm happy that you haven't touched your glasses today. You always seem to be cleaning, even when it isn't dirty. Thank goodness you haven't touched the poor thing today." Andrew said laughing on the grass while Cassy threw a friendly punch at him.

I had just finished helping with the dishes when I heard my phone ring. I dried my hands and ran to the living room to grab it. I didn't want to miss the call. Then I answered the call,

"Hello, Mr. Joe Bryan. How are you doing? "

" I am doing fine, Katy. Can I talk with you, Katy? It won't take long but it's important "

"Okay, can we meet at the park, 4:30 pm?"

"Oh sure, we can. Thanks, Katy. See you at the park."

I couldn't even guess what topic Mr. Joe Bryan wanted to talk about but the fact that he said it was important, I knew it was a big deal.

I told mom that I was going out for a ride with my bike to see Mr. Joe Bryan.

"Alright, Sweetie. Ride safely, stay off the main road, and come back early for dinner. Mom replied while I walked off. Mr. Joe Bryan's car pulled up right about the same time that I wheeled my bicycle into the park. We both were right on time. I shook hands with him while we sat under a tree. I could hear the distant cry of a bird tweeting high above the trees. Asides from that, every other part of the park seemed quiet. The activities reduced after the plane crashed into the park.

"So, you wanted to see me, Mr. Joe. Any problem?"

"Do you care for a drink? I could go grab two cups of lemonade over the lemonade stand."

"No thanks, I'm fine."

I noticed Mr. Bryan kept on interlocking his two fingers while he spoke. He then went ahead to ask about Tina and what he said made me raise both of my brows in awe,

"Katy. I've been thinking about the little girl, Tina ever since you spoke about her the last time we met and how she had lost both her parents. My wife and I have been married for a while now, but we have never been parents. We've tried everything possible but it's just not working. When you mentioned Tina that day, my heart felt drawn to her even though I haven't met her. My wife and I would like to adopt Tina."

"Wow! I didn't see this coming Mr. Joe. Wow! This is the best news I've heard in a long, long time. So, Tina is going to have new parents?" I asked and Mr. Joe nodded. I told him that my buddies and I were going over to the glasshouse to see how the people there were faring.

"You could come along with us so that you'd get to see Tina," I told Mr. Bryan.

"Katy, my wife, and I have been to the glasshouse to make inquiries about the adoption process. I met with the coordinator of the children, Miss. Grace and she's been a great help, but we haven't met Tina yet."

'Oh, wow that's a good one. I am happy you are making progress already." I replied smiling as if my lips were going to expand. I just couldn't contain my joy.

"I'd come to pick you and the other guys at your house whatever time you pick."

"That would be so cool. We'd be expecting you."

We stood up to go, the cooing overhead had seized, and silence once again fell upon the entire park. Mr. Joe Bryan was already in his car, about to drive off when we both sighted Andrew sitting in the flower section of the garden. Mr. Joe Bryan and I went over to meet him, and Andrew had a flush of pink on his cheeks when he saw us. We all greeted; Mr. Joe Bryan told Andrew how sorry he was about his mom's demise. Andrew just nodded his head, faked a smile, and said he was grateful.

"Thank you so much, Mr. Joe Bryan. Your decision means a lot to me. Thank you." I hugged Mr. Joe Bryan before he stepped into his car. I stayed back to keep Andrew's company. I expected him to ask about what decision I was speaking about with Mr. Bryan, but he just kept his eyes fixed on the white daffodils, sprinkled across the fields. Dannie would surely have asked about the decision if he were to be here. That evening, I spent the entire time talking with Andrew and it was the best feeling ever. I blushed a few times, but my cheeks turned bright red when Andrew and I held hands as we walked down the flowery sidewalk. He also came with his bicycle and together, we raced home.

That night as I lay down to sleep, beautiful memories of the day's events flashed through my mind and spread a wide smile across my lips. First off, Tina was going to have new parents. I told mom about it the moment I returned home, and she seemed excited about the news too. I knew that Tina was going to love and accept the Bryans. I had a good feeling about the whole adoption stuff.

Second and the most beautiful memory of that day was the fact that I could spend time with Andrew in a relaxed environment. Andrew did tell me about his mom and how much he missed her. He unlocked the room of grief inside his heart and allowed the pain to flow out. He cried a few times and I hugged him, patting his back while he spilled tears all over my shoulder. But I didn't mind. I was glad that Andrew was letting it all out. I knew he was going to be just fine. I drifted to sleep with the memory of my hands locked with that of Andrews'. No doubt, Andrew and I were getting along on a whole new level. It was the best feeling ever.

Mr. Bryan and his wife did come to pick us up at my house and together we headed for the glasshouse. Mr. Bryan's wife had a face that could turn many heads around. Her eyes were the zenith of her beauty, almond-shaped, and perfect for her round face. I knew that Tina was going to like her. When we arrived at the glasshouse, my eyes went on an immediate search for Tina. Cassy, Dannie, and Andrew started visiting different compartments of the glasshouse. We planned that we all were going to talk about peace and harmony in the glasshouse. I kept on with my search for Tina while Mr. And Mrs. Bryan stood at the entrance of the glasshouse. Mrs. Bryan seemed nervous as she clutched her husband's hands tightly.

I finally found Tina with Miss Grace and I hugged Tina warmly. Miss Grace said she had been away trying to make Tina look her best because of the visitors coming over to see her. Miss Grace surely did transform Tina and she looked more beautiful than she had ever been. Her hair was packed into two buns and knotted with ribbons. She had a flowery dress on and a matching shoe that made her look so cute. Tina smiled when I held her in my arms as we walked over to Bryan's. Mrs. Bryan reached out to Tina and the little girl didn't even resist the embrace of the woman. Tears slid down my face as Tina rested her head on Mrs. Bryan's chest and Mr. Bryan embraced both as tears moistened his eyes. I was happy to see that Tina had accepted her new parents. Miss Grace also had some tears to spill. She said that Tina had been more than lively, ever since she told her that she was going to leave the glasshouse.

I went over to meet the buddies while Bryan's stayed with Tina. DACK began going from one compartment to the other, telling the people to love themselves and help each other out no matter what happens. We also told them about the pod and the incoming flood but assured them that we all were going to be safe. We shared cookies, sweets, and chocolates with the children. It was fun seeing smiles on the faces of children in the glasshouse. It was worth it.

The day that the pod was finally completed, one would have thought that it was the Independence Day celebration. It was all over the news and press conferences. An eagle view of the whole pod was taken from a drone and displayed on the news. It was a huge house, large enough to envelop the whole city and everything in it. Similar pods built in other cities were also shown on the news and the structures truly looked magnificent. It was a beauty to witness.

"Today, as we mark the completion of the pod, we are delighted to see that the plan B project pulled through. Millions of dollars have been sunk into the project, but it's nothing compared to the safety of lives, properties, animals, and the whole ecosystem. The floods and sea levels might invade any moment from now, but we are not afraid because the pod is there to protect us. Fishing activities would continue even though we are in the pod. Special fishing instruments designed to pass through the pod material would be used to harvest fish from the surrounding water to feed the population. We have come a long way together; we would continue to help one another. Long live humanity!" The Administrator of Environment had stated on the news.

The buddies and I launched a peace campaign around the city just to inform people that unity had brought us where we are. We went about with the STF vests we had and told people to live in peace. DACK wasn't just a team, we had become peace advocates too, telling people that cooperation, love, and peace would keep us united.

"We humans aren't just successful because of strength or larger brains that we possess but we are successful because of the way we help each other out," Dannie explained during one of our peace campaigns. We had other kids join our revolution, as we began to proclaim peace and harmony wherever we went. Andrew took the video clips of us during our peace walks and we posted them on the web for other cities to see and learn. DACK was given an award of excellence to honor us for our service to the whole flood intervention and volunteering services. We were the youngest volunteers on the STF board, and we were given awards for making our own little contribution to the flood.

Tina had already moved in with the Bryans and she was officially Tina Bryan. I stopped over at Bryan's house to see older, Mrs. Bryan and she had Tina in the warmth of her hands. They both looked happy while in each other's embrace. Mrs. Bryan gave me a gentle squeeze and stated that she was happy to have the feeling of being a grandmother. I was happy that I had found a home for Tina.

On one very cold, windy morning, the floods did arrive, but I remained warm under my comforter even amidst the violent storm outside. Water was indeed the beginning of the end. The end to disunity and the beginning of peace, love, and cooperation.

Chapter Twelve

I felt the sun's rays tickle my face when my eyes fluttered open. There was a yawn hanging in my mouth and I stifled it out, stretching my arms and wriggling my toes. it was 7:00 am when my eyes caught the tick of the clock. Damn! I was already late for school. DACK and the entire class were going on a tour around the outskirts of the city. The pod surrounded the city's borders and since it was a crystal clear, see-through housing, it would be easier to see the fishes and the level of the water. We wanted to see the waters and how high the sea levels had risen. It was all Dannie's idea. The news report had stated that some houses situated around the borders of the city could see fishes moving in the water from the pod. That report had provoked Dannie so much, he couldn't stop chatting about it when we met at the cafeteria that day.

"Hey buddies, you know we could go on a tour to the outskirts of the city to go see some fishes. I bet they would be in their numbers now that the water had risen. It would be so much fun." Dannie said with creases of laughter all over his face.

"Well, that sounds like a good idea but how do we go about it?" Cassy replied squinting her eyes as she just looked at the sun. Her glasses broke the day before and her face seemed so bland without them.

"We could suggest to Mrs. Helen. Let's make it a class thing, that way we would be safe and under supervision." Andrew said.

I hurried off to the bathroom like I was being followed. Dannie and I were going to lead the entire team of the class together with other teachers. I couldn't afford to be late.

Ever since DACK had uploaded videos about peace and cooperation, a lot of kids had decided to be a part of our team. It was like a dream come true to see young kids interested in developing goals to unite people. Finally, I was making an impact in my own little way. DACK became really popular at school and we had a say. Teachers began to involve us in extracurricular activities, and we formed a club, "peace and unity group". It wasn't so difficult to talk Mrs. Helen into allowing us to go for the tour and our request was granted. The announcement was made to the class by Dannie and we are scheduled to visit the following morning.

It was Andrew's voice that bellowed in my ears just when I got off my mom's car.

"Katy, where have you been? We have been waiting for you the whole time!"

"I'm sorry, I slept way more than I expected," I told Andrew while we both hurried to the bus. It was packed full of students and teachers.

"I am sorry everyone!" I exclaimed when I got on the bus. There were murmurs after I spoke, but Dannie's voice soon quieted the bus while he stated the purpose of the tour and spelled out the rules.

I took a seat beside Cassy. She looked completely different; one would have thought there was a new girl at school. If not for her voice, I wouldn't have known it was her all along while I sat beside her.

"Katy you are late! Your eyes look like you haven't slept in years. You were chatting late into the night with Andrew yeah? " Cassy replied with low tones and a small frown.

I stifled a laugh before answering her. "Not exactly, Cassy. Yeah, I did talk with Andrew on phone, but that wasn't what kept me awake. I was just too excited about the tour, I couldn't sleep. Cassy, you look like a new girl at school! I couldn't even recognize you. You have been squinting all the while too. I think I prefer the 'four-eyed Cassy than the two-eyed one. You should go get them as soon as possible girl."

"Katy, I told you my glasses got broken a few days back. It's still undergoing repairs and I'm getting new frames. My face feels so naked right now." Cassy replied with her hands on her face. I gave her a warm squeeze and she smiled back with a more relaxed look. I loved Cassy with or without her glasses and nothing was going to change that.

The outskirts of the city looked like a transparent film from the pod. We already began to see the height of the water even before the bus came to a halt. Seeing the water outside of the pod made me cringe but I smiled even as the hair on my skin stood erect as I know that I was safe in the confines of the pod. I remembered the nightmares I had of being buried six feet beneath the grip of water, grappling for breath. The feeling of the nightmares returned as I stared at the mass of water swaying back and forth. Some students like Dannie seemed so excited and elated while other students fell silent when we got off the bus. Mrs. Helen led the way while we filed to the extreme of the pod's wall. There were some men in uniform guarding the place, but we were allowed to go close enough to the transparent wall.

Dannie talked about the material used to make the pod and students placed their faces close to the wall to see the water. I traced invisible patterns on the walls of the pod while I looked through. That event reminded me of the glasshouse and how the buddies and I used to trace our hands on the walls of the glasshouse and draw various diagrams on it. While I stood in front of the pod wall, Andrew came and stood beside me. His hands then locked with mine. Earlier when I entered the bus looking all puffy-eyed and tired, Andrew had winked at me and that pulled a string in my heart. I smiled back at him and he smiled back too. Now that we were holding hands, we had ample time to talk. Andrew had just removed a speck of dirt from my hair when we heard the brunette girl in the class yell.

"Over here! Over here!! I can see a fish. Over here, everyone!"

We dashed to where the brunette girl was, and she pointed to where she had seen the fish. The fish wasn't in sight, but the excitement written all over her face was proof that she really saw a fish. We all stayed glued to the wall of the pod when suddenly, the fish emerged with shiny black skin. It looked like a baby dolphin and it came close to the pod and splashed water all over. Some students freaked out when the fish came close, but Dannie and the brunette girl stayed with eyes glued on the fish. Even Mrs. Helen stood a few meters away from the pod's wall, she seemed a bit scared too. When we began clapping and yelling the fish vanished out of sight back into the water. That was the most memorable event of that day and after sharing peanuts and lemonade, we all boarded the bus and returned to school. Guys took photos of the fish in the water and we all looked at the photographs. The fish didn't have scales and so it wasn't hunted but one of the guards had told us that the fishermen had begun fishing with special instruments through the walls of the pod. This time on our way back, I sat close to Andrew and we talked to our heart's content all the way back.

It was a Saturday, bright and beautiful like every other morning. I was eating breakfast while dad was working on his system and mom was busy gardening, we had no clue about what was happening. I had just mouthed a spoon full of cereal when Dannie's text message beeped on my phone.

"Morning Katy. Have you seen the news yet?" My eyes quickly read through the message while I made for the stairs. Dad was on the couch with his system. I immediately turned on the TV without even saying a word. I was eager to hear what the news had to say. Dannie's text had a disturbing tone. I knew something was up. There it was on the news update.

"Glasshouse housing over hundreds of people crashes to the ground."

I stood transfixed as my feet stayed glued to the ground. My mind raced back and forth searching through the memories of the people I knew in the glasshouse, especially Miss Grace. Tina seemed like she was the only friend I had in the glasshouse back then, but I had become fond of some of the folks there. I might not even say a word to some of them during our STF outreaches, but the warmth of their eyes does envelope me with serenity. I couldn't imagine losing anyone in the glasshouse or have them injured. The voice of the news correspondent answered my wandering thoughts and questions, as she stated that no life was lost but many were injured and they were undergoing medical care already.

The cause of the glasshouse collapse wasn't known yet. Some said some kids in the glasshouse had started breaking some parts of the glasshouse while playing, others speculated that maybe the trapped sunlight heating the pod had affected the glasshouse, causing cracks in different places. Whatever the cause was, it was a disaster that had rendered thousands of people homeless, including children. The STF scheme had also set out to visit the site. The buddies and I along with other volunteer students were all set out to visit the place too. When we got there, I couldn't believe that this was the same glasshouse we had stayed in, years earlier. Everything was reduced to a rubble of shattered glass pieces. Some people were still hanging around the place as they didn't have anywhere to go. When I asked of Miss Grace, I was told she was part of those in the hospital. I could only hope that she would be safe and wasn't badly injured.

That night when I got home, sleep had taken a vacation from my eyes. All I could see when I closed my eyes were the rumbles of shredded glass and the homeless boys and girls sitting in front of the 'once upon a time' magnificent glasshouse. Other glasshouses in other cities were still standing tall and sturdy. I couldn't figure the reason why this particular glasshouse had to crumple. "Well, it is what it is," I muttered to myself under the sheets. As sleep finally came around, the last memory I had was that of Tina. I couldn't imagine her under the rumbles of the glasshouse. But she was safe in the hands of Bryan's and that pulled a huge smile on my face even as I drifted to sleep.

I was awakened by the noise of unrest the next morning. I got out of bed and peeped out of the window, only to see hundreds of people scattered on the streets.

Various placards and cardboards of different colors danced above their heads as they trailed past. I figured that they must be those who were once housed in the glasshouse. The pod was the only hope now. Many children roamed the streets. I ran down the stairs, I could hear the blasting sirens all over the place. That means the crowd was beginning to get out of hand, I guessed.

When I got to the living room, mom and dad were already glued to the news, they didn't notice when I took a seat beside them. The government had stated that they weren't expecting this kind of an internal disaster at this point in time. They however stated that they would begin to find another alternative for the homeless. In the meantime, a temporary shelter would be erected at the park to accommodate people.

"Dad, I actually didn't think that the glasshouse would fail at any time. Imagine if we all had relied solely on the glasshouse. We would have been swept away even before the water increased."

"Yeah, Katy. You are correct. It was a wise decision that the government embraced the construction of the pod around cities. I can't imagine if the glass walls around the city had collapsed. We would be like fishes dancing and swimming in the flood by now."

"The pod is our only hope now. I just hope an alternative is provided at the soonest to curb the social unrest of those on the street." Mom said before dashing into the kitchen.

The buddies and I visited the alternative shelter on our way back from school. When we got there, it was packed full to the brim. Dannie couldn't help but open his mouth ajar when he saw that the once, quiet and serene park had become a beehive of activities.

"I guess STF has a lot of work to do now more than ever" Cassy replied adjusting her new, round glasses. They seemed to fit better than the previous ones she had on.

"That's right. The STF coordinator already texted me that we should prepare to distribute relief materials to homeless people. I'd announce on the class page so that other students can volunteer to assist us." I replied.

The relief distribution wasn't an easy task at all, but we all had committed to the service of STF and to ensure peace and unity among people. That had become our watchword and so even during the distribution exercise, DACK and other young buddies made it a point to preach peace among the people. We also assured them that the government was working hard to provide an alternative that would once again serve as a home for the homeless.

Chapter Thirteen

"Hello, Katy. Wake up, it's me."

"You, who?"

"Call me whatever name you choose but I have just started with you guys. I ain't going down the drain anytime soon."

"Who are you? What do you want from me?"

"It's me, Katy. You know me and I know you. Katy! Katy!! Katy!!!!..."

I yanked out of bed with a scream when I woke up to mom's gentle voice calling my name. Mom had been calling my name the whole time, but I couldn't even hear her voice. I was so afraid in my nightmare, my hair stood erect when I woke up. I was thankful it was just a dream.

"What happened to you, Katy? Did you see a ghost in your sleep? You don't look alright at all sweetheart. Want some coffee?"

"No, I'm fine mom, it's just a nightmare, nothing more. I'd be alright." I replied mom in between pants. My pajamas looked like it had just gone under the shower. Well, it's my sweat, I woke up in a pool of salty liquid.

"Well. You'd be fine honey. Just get dressed and get ready, remember it's a big day for you. By the time you are done freshening up, breakfast would be sitting on the table. I'm actually gonna brew some coffee for you. You sure need it." mom replied and planted a kiss on my forehead before leaving the room.

It sure was a big day for me, but I didn't feel it. My nightmare seemed to have sapped every pint of energy reserve that I had bubbling in me. I thought the nightmare had taken a break from showing up in my sleep, but it didn't look like it. I had just squeezed an ample amount of paste on my toothbrush when the nightmare suddenly made sense to me. It was water that had paid me a visit in my dream. It was water that said it knew me and I knew it. "Water just wasn't done yet. That means there might be some more flooding." I muttered to myself, my mouth now full of the minty toothpaste.

The government had successfully concluded the alternate shelter for the homeless. Since the whole city was secured in the confines of the pod, there wasn't a need for any glasshouses anymore. The alternative shelter was built with simple materials like concrete and bricks large enough to house hundreds of people. It had various compartmental like those in the previous glasshouse. The STF team had decided to visit the shelter and help people settle there. That was the big day I had ahead of me, and I felt spent even before the day's activities began. I munched on my cookies quietly while mom drove me to the alternate shelter. I couldn't wait to tell the buddies about my nightmare. They were the only ones that could relate to what I was going through.

Later that day, we helped a few people settle down in their compartments and my heart was warmed to see smiles back on the faces of people again. These were the same faces that wore gloom and despair a few months back when the glasshouse had crumbled. They were the same faces that were screaming on the streets to get the governments' attention to provide alternate housing. I was thankful that the government had granted their plea at last. The children's compartment even had toys littered all over the place just to make them comfy and happy. STF buses were done conveying people from the park down to the alternative shelter. We were all fatigued but fulfilled. It was a long, hectic day indeed.

Dannie was the first to speak up when we were about to have our lunch break at the shelter.

"Katy, you were talking about the nightmare you had last night when we arrived this morning. What's it about?" Dannie asked with a serious look on his face. He always wore this look on whenever he had something important to discuss.

" Yeah, buddies. I had a nightmare last night and I saw water talking to me. I was..."

"Woah, Woah! Hold on Katy. I know you have been having a series of nightmares in the past but this one sounds absolutely ridiculous. Water isn't a being you know. Have you been watching some sci-fi movies lately?" Cassy's voice cut in sharply.

"Well, not really. The whole point is that I knew I saw water; it doesn't matter if it makes sense to you guys or not. I just know that water ain't going down anytime soon. There might be further cases of flooding in the nearest future. I mean we are all in a pod yeah, we are safe and all but are we going to continue living like this, jumping from one hurdle to the other? I wish there's something we could do to put an end to the rising sea levels. I just wish there was a permanent way out of this whole water menace."

"Hmmm. Well, Katy, I know how you feel. I sometimes wish we could relocate to another planet entirely. I sometimes freak out when I imagine my 101 children being birthed in the confines of a pod. It gives me goosebumps." Andrew's reply made us all laugh amidst the heat of the discussion and that lightened the atmosphere a bit. We went further to talk about the possibility of even relocating to another planet as Andrew had suggested. Dannie had suggested Mars, Andrew said Jupiter while Cassy and I laughed almost all through the conversation. All other planets didn't seem to be habitable. It turned out to be a "planet game" that we were playing before the STF coordinator called us to come round off the last stage of our duties. That night before I got into my pajamas, I penned down the possibility of relocating to another planet in my geography journal. The very thought of it intrigued me. I made up my mind that I wasn't going to hesitate to visit other planets if I ever got the chance. With that thought in mind, I hurried off to floss, fantasizing about the adventures that existed on other planets.

I was brushing Kula's brown fur and the dog wagged in satisfaction as the brush-stroked her back gently. I had just finished wiping off the droplets of water that spilled on the floor when dad called me.

"Just a minute dad." I hurried up the stairs with Kula on my trail. Dad told me that he had been trying to place a call through to one of his friends, but he wasn't getting any signal at all. He wanted to know if my phone had a signal too. I hurried to get my phone and it couldn't even send a text or voice message too. The signal bar wasn't even showing up on my phone's screen.

"This is strange. It has never happened before plus the Wi-Fi in the house has been strong of late. Why the sudden change this afternoon? " dad asked with a puzzled look on his face. I tried to place a call through to my buddies, but it was futile. Dad and I decided to go on a stroll down the street to see if the network would pick up. Mom had gone to get groceries and her line wasn't going through too. When dad and I stepped on the front deck of the house, we were amazed at what we saw. There were quite a few people on the street, all hanging their phones in the air as if they were flying a kite. Everyone seemed to be trying to get a signal into their phones. Some had their laptops and

IPads in the air too. They are like chicken littles on the street.

I sighted Mr. John sitting in his car with his laptop on his thigh. He was the closest neighbor that lived across our house. I had never seen any other person come out of his house, no woman or children. His place always seemed quiet. He never smiled, and his expression was always bland, you couldn't predict anything from his expressions. Dad went down the street to talk with a few of them, while I went across to talk with Mr. John. I knocked on the window of his car while he wound down and sent a cold stare at me, but his voice wasn't anything close to cold. His voice wore a calm, quiet tone.

"Hey, Mr. John. Sorry to bother you but do you have any signal on your laptop? I noticed that it's on."

"No Katy. I just left it on just in case a signal would sweep by. The network has been crazy for the past hour. I sat in the car hoping that the signal would improve. I was surprised to see the entire neighborhood on the street. I guess it's a general problem." He replied squinting his eyes. They look deprived of sleep. I thanked him and headed for the house. Dad was still talking with other neighbors. Mom's car pulled into the driveway just when I was about to enter the house.

"Welcome back mom. How was your drive back home?"

"Thanks, sweetie. A lot of people littered the road on my way back. There were a lot of phones hanging in the air. I then picked up my phone to place a call through to your dad. That was when I realized that there was no signal at all. I think there's a problem again."

I grabbed the groceries from the backseat and headed for the house. While mom was busy in the kitchen, all I could think of was that we had another hurdle to cross over. But this one seemed like the mother of all hurdles. I couldn't imagine life without the media.

The sun was retiring to bed and so were we. Yet, the signal hadn't returned to our phones and even the cable is down. We couldn't see any Tv and I knew that this problem was real. As I drifted to sleep, I wondered what new plan would come up as the days strolled by.

Social unrest soon took over the streets again after one week of no internet or television signals. It looked like we had lived a whole year without any signal as each day seemed too sluggish for the next. The newspaper was now the only hope of recent news and happenings around. It was a boom to the printing press economy because people were itching to know the recent happenings. A telecommunications expert as I read in the newspaper had stated that the communication systems are having issues due to the rising sea levels.

"Radio waves do not travel well in water and that is exactly what is happening now. The rising sea levels have taken hold of the electromagnetic waves and that has caused a ripple effect on our telecommunications systems. We were continually improving and adapting the communication systems to the new environments in the last few years. However, this time the water seems to be one step ahead of us. We, therefore, plead everyone to stay calm as we are seriously working round the clock to ensure that the systems are restored." Said the expert in the newspaper.

I couldn't imagine a world devoid of the media and other means of communication. It was like living in a desert. The protest returned to the streets and some people couldn't even be tamed. The Police, FBI, and other security agencies soon took over the streets too to tame and calm down wild protesters. Teenagers weren't left out in the protests too. Schoolwork became a burden as we couldn't access the internet and even classes became boring. Life suddenly became useless outside technology.

When it looked like all hope was lost, a spark of hope flickered in the darkness of our hurdle. A particular satellite was able to communicate in the city's stadium a few times a day. It wasn't really strong, but it was enough to pull a call through and could also allow basic internet browsing. But the population was too large for such a weak signal at the stadium, hence the government came up with a plan. It was Mrs. Helen that broke the news to us during our lunch break at the cafeteria,

"We teachers had a meeting with the government two days ago and there's a plan. Since the signal at the stadium isn't going to cater to the population, special satellite devices would be distributed amongst teachers. Those satellite devices would transmit information from happenings around the world and we, in turn, would relay this information to those around us. That way, we would be able to share information with the crowd. To this effect, we would need volunteers to assist us in communicating this information. Other organizations would have representatives that would be given these satellite devices to also transmit information to their workers too. That way, we would be able to curb social unrest. So, who's in?" Mrs. Helen asked and DACK and other students raised their hands to volunteer.

I wasn't surprised when the plan didn't work out because I knew that it would fail from the very beginning. It worked out well in the first week. Teachers read out the news to students from their satellite devices at the stadium, some individuals even got signal into their personal computers and laptops, but the unrest returned. People began to complain that driving to the stadium each day wasn't convenient and teachers began to complain of being fatigued too. When we arrived at the stadium the following morning, there were no signals at the stadium. Now, it dawned on me that we were probably going to be cut off from every form of communication in the days to come.

The last time we went to the stadium, DACK decided to brainstorm ideas of how the communication satellite could be restored with other bright minds from other high schools. Great ideas did show up. It was a plump, blonde that came up with the idea that might work. She seemed quiet while we were conversing. She wore glasses similar to those of Cassy and I smiled when she adjusted her glasses before speaking in her high-pitched voice.

"How about we build underground tunnels that can establish communication and connectivity between other podded cities? You know other cities are in a pod too, but they still have working communication systems. We could link up with them and connect with their communication networks through underground tunnels. It may take quite a bit of time to dig up these tunnels, but I don't think we have a choice. We need to bring all the smartest engineers in the city together to plan this tunnel. I think this is possible." She said with confidence.

Dannie was the first to start clapping when the girl was done talking and others followed suit. I later got to know her name was Suzy and she soon became my friend. I introduced Suzy to the STF coordinator, she soon became a part of the volunteers. We relayed our suggestion to the STF team, and they took it to the government officials.

We were surprised to see the work commence immediately, as our suggestion was approved. All thanks to Suzy, there was finally a way out of the hurdle. Andrew stated that Suzy became a part of DACK.

"And so, we are now three girls against two boys," Cassy replied, skipping around with laughter during our official hang out with our new member, Suzy. We were now five teens on a mission to lead other teens in changing the world. DACKS had come to stay.

It took a while, but the engineers came up with a smart way to excavate by using mining technology to blast huge chunks of soil at a time and they built giant industrial vacuums to extract all the debris. The piles of dirt were distributed throughout the city. These huge underground tunnels were as large as 8 lane highways and 200 meters deep underground. They build wired communication systems like the ones used decades ago but it is still effective. It took a year before the connected pods brought back the internet and information from other podded cities with them. It felt like we are all living in ant colonies. It has become the new normal.

Chapter Fourteen

Mom couldn't get out of bed. Every other day, she would be the first to peek at my bedroom door and plant a kiss on my forehead. She's been doing that ever since I was a child and never stopped even when I turned eighteen, but this morning was an exception. I was at her bedside and she was shivering under the covers. I stroked her black, lush hair that had streaks of grey strands in it while her eyes opened and closed intermittently. Dad was away on a two-day trip in another part of town, so it was just mom and me at home. She had complained about having slight body aches the night before, but she was in an awfully bad shape this morning. Her body temperature could even fry an egg.

"Mom, care for some coffee? I could brew some for you. Maybe it would help relax your nerves. You are burning up already. We should see a doctor mom."

"No, Katy. I'm alright. I just wanna sleep okay? I'd be fine." Mom muttered faintly. I had to strain my ears to make sense of what she said. I covered her gently and patted her head before leaving her room. Kula whimpered somewhere around the room and I shooed her out with me, so she wouldn't crawl beside mom. I called dad as I was leaving the room, but he was not picking up. Ever since the interconnectivity between pods had been established, there had been stable communication and the network has been good. I wondered why dad wasn't picking up. Worry had begun to creep in.

Andrew's call pulled through when I dialed his number and the moment, I heard his voice, tears welled up in my eyes. The day the stars were shining at their brightest, the day we all dressed up in our beautiful dresses and suits for prom night, was the same day that Andrew asked me out to be his girlfriend. I wasn't so surprised because we had become so fond of ourselves in recent times. I said yes and that night was the same night I locked lips with Andrew for the first time. Cassy, Dannie, and Suzy were there to cheer us up while we had our first kiss. Dating Andrew has been a sweet ride and he always showed up when I needed him the most.

"Hello Andrew, good morning."

"Hey, babe. Good morning. Your voice sounds like you gonna tear up anytime soon. What's the problem?"

"I'm kinda fine but mom's not fine, Drew. She has been restless all morning and I don't know what to do. Dad isn't at home too. I'm worried about mom." I replied in between sobs.

"'Calm down baby, just calm down. Mom is gonna be fine, okay, and just stay strong. You will be fine. I'd be with you shortly. Take care. See you soon."

I clicked off the phone and smiled a bit. I knew that Andrew was going to come as he had said, and I couldn't wait to get into his embrace. The warmth of his embrace always made me feel secure.

The US government and other visionaries of the world had begun to coordinate and come together to fight the common menace, water. The sea levels were rising by the minute and environmental experts had predicted that within the next ten years, the whole earth could be submerged in the grip of water. NGOs affiliated with climate change had also begun to enlighten people about possible outcomes of the flood and its effect on the earth in the next ten years. The news of planet relocation to save humanity was under consideration but I knew deep within me that it was going to be the only way out. Planet Relocation and Revolution Scheme (PRRS) was initiated and inaugurated by the US government and their sole aim together with other countries of the world was to implement ways by which humanity could be salvaged and become interplanetary beings.

I had just finished my usual online read up on happenings around the world and surfing the internet when a mail popped up in my mailbox. I rubbed my eyes and stifled a yawn before opening the mail. By the time I read the content of the mail, every pint of sleep had evaded my eyes and anyone who saw me at that moment could see the pink bloom on my cheeks even in the dark.

"Dear Katy,

It is with great delight that I send you this mail. My team and I are fully aware of what you are doing as a DACKS team. We have been following your Peace campaigns online and have seen your videos. We would love your team to partner with us as we have the same goal, which is to create awareness about the happenings around the world and how humanity can live in peace and cooperation during this crisis. My NGO just got affiliated with the PRRS and together, we would enlighten as many as we can on the need to save the world and the prospects of surviving on another planet. It would be a pleasure to work with young minds. I await a favorable response from you. Thank you.

Best Regards,

Brenda."

Brenda. That name rang a bell in my memory. Yes! I remembered. It was the same Brenda that led the campaign of young farmers during the food crisis, years back. After watching that campaign that day, I quickly looked up Brenda and her team online and I had been following all her online posts and liked every one of her comments and articles. She was one of the people I looked up to, right from when I was much younger and even more now. When the communications were interrupted, I lost contact with Brenda and got so busy, I didn't even remember to look up her profile again. Now that her mail was sitting in my mailbox, I could only smile as she reached out to me personally. I couldn't wait to share the good news with my buddies. DACKS and team were going global.

There was a buzz in my ears that made me suddenly jump out of bed. I thought it was another nightmare until I realized it was my phone ringing loudly. I stretched from side to side and yawned loudly before answering Cassy's call. I couldn't believe it was morning already. The night seemed short.

"Damn! It's just seven in the morning Cassy and you are already on the phone. Don't you sleep at all?"

"Rise and shine sleepy head. Good morning to you. I know it's seven in the morning and you should have gotten your ass out of bed by now. Anyway, I couldn't wait till we saw each other that's why I called this early. Your text message was the first thing I read when I woke up. Girl! I am so happy about this. Partnering with a huge Environmental expert like Brenda and her entire team is a big win. I've been smiling all morning."

"Yeah Casey. It is a big win indeed. You needed to see the way my cheeks were glowing when her mail came in. I couldn't even wait till our hangout that's why I texted you guys immediately after replying to Brenda's mail."

"Yeah. That's a good one. We are making progress. Don't forget to be on time at the hangout girl. Remember it's 5:00 pm at the park."

"I know Cassy. Thank you. I gotta go now and catch some sweet sleep. It's an early Saturday morning and I got to sleep some more. Take care girl. See ya soon. Bye."

I've cut the call before Cassy even said goodbye. I needed to sleep before facing the day's activities. I didn't even know how I woke up from the bed. The night before, I dozed off on the chair after texting my friends. Waking up on the bed wasn't a total mystery though. Maybe dad had tucked me in bed while he was checking around the house as was his routine while we all slept. This wasn't the first or the second time I would sleep on the chair and wake on the bed and dad was always the one to the rescue. I covered myself under the sheets to continue my long sleep while the birds continued tweeting outside my window. The weather looked cheerful, so was I.

I applied a light red lipstick on, and it made a matching combo with the red flowers printed on my shirt. My hair was packed in a bun as always and I was tying the lace on my sneakers when mom's voice echoed from the sitting room.

"Hurry up honey, it's almost 4:00 pm. You are running late already. Don't keep your buddies waiting."

"Yes, mom. I'm almost done. I'd be downstairs in a minute." I brushed my hair one more time and wore my favorite perfume on before hurrying down the stairs. I planted a kiss on mom's head and hugged dad before picking up the car keys on the table.

"That reminds me, dad, did you come by my room in the night? I remember dozing off on the chair, but I woke on the bed."

"Sure, I was. When I was doing my normal night routine I stopped by and noticed your lamp was still on. So, I knocked, got in when I didn't hear a response, and noticed you were asleep, and I tucked you in."

"Thanks, dad. I got to go now. It won't be that long. Take care of mom."

I heard mom say "Bye, sweetie," before I ran out of the door. As I drove on to the park, my mind drifted back to the day mom was seriously ill. When Andrew showed up that day, I immediately fell into his embrace and spilled my tears on his neck while he stroked my back gently. We both took mom to the hospital that day and I heaved a sigh of relief when the doctors stated that mom was ill due to accumulated stress. She was given medication. Dad and I ensured that she rested from all her duties in the house, while I helped out. Now that she was getting better, I could relax. It was Suzy's voice that garnered my thoughts back to reality as I pulled my car to a halt in the park's driveway. Suzy's house was just a few blocks away from the park, so she was always the first to show up.

"Hey, Katy. That's a beautiful shirt you have on. You look gorgeous by the way. Is someone going on a date?" Suzy teased as we walked together through the park's entrance.

"Cut it out, Suzy. I didn't even have a date in mind. I just wanted to dress up. I've been so elated since I got Brenda's mail."

"Yeah, that's true. That's huge progress." Suzy replied. We met Dannie when we got to our usual spot.

"Hey, Dannie. Good to see you. Where is Cassy by the way?"

"Hi, Katy. Cassy went off to get some drinks for us down the street. She should be here soon. Where's Andrew? He should be here by now. I've never known him to be late for the meeting. I thought you guys were going to come together."

"Well, I thought I was going to meet him here too. When we spoke earlier today, he didn't tell me he would be running late. Maybe something came up or he would have got held up in traffic."

Andrew arrived at the same time as Cassy and he winked at me while we all exchanged pleasantries. When Dannie asked Andrew why he was late, with his hair and shirt ruffled, he explained that his car had refused to start and when he realized he was running late, he biked down to the park. He didn't even realize how messy he looked till we told him.

I opened the meeting by congratulating DACKS for partnering with Brenda and her team and we talked about possible ways of enlightening the public about the PRRS. Dannie suggested that we hold a rally and subsequent campaigns to get more teens on board. He stated that many youngsters were awaiting summer before going to college, just like we were and that the campaign would be a means of getting them busy. Everyone agreed to Dannie's idea but Suzy. She cringed before speaking up,

"Well, talking about college I usually wonder if we would ever be going to college or if we would ever have a future before the water consumes us. I know I'm not meant to be saying these because we have to proffer hope to people and all, but I just get scared sometimes." Suzy replied gently as the sun's rays cast shadows on her glasses. We could see fear buried in her eyes as she raised her head gently.

"Don't worry Suzy. We all have our little fears about what the future holds and if this planet relocation scheme would ever work out, but we have to be optimistic and always remind ourselves that we must survive no matter what happens. Don't worry about it. We all will be fine." Dannie said and patted Suzy's back gently. When Suzy calmed, Cassy assigned roles to us to help out in the preparation of the forthcoming rally: I was assigned to call Brenda and invite her for our next meeting before the rally. Cassy and Suzy were to contact friends and classmates to invite them to the rally. While Dannie and Andrew were in charge of all protocol arrangements. After we dispersed, I was on my way to the car when I felt a hand wrap around my waist. Andrew's scent enveloped my senses as he whispered into my ears and kissed my neck gently.

"You look so gorgeous Katy; I couldn't help steal glances from your face all through the meeting."

"Thanks, babe. We should go on a date from here you know."

"No Katy, I am too shabby to sit beside a dazzling beauty like you. My hair is ruffled and there are grease stains on my trousers. We could go some other time babe."

"I love you any day, anytime, shabby or not and I want us to go out today. A cup of coffee isn't such a bad idea after all." I whispered into Andrew's ears before locking my lips with his. All the elements of the universe seemed still even as Andrew kissed me. It was the best feeling in the world. Suzy's hunch was right. I was going on a date with my Andrew.

Chapter Fifteen

It was all over the news headlines. Drones couldn't even fly outside the pod anymore. Scientists had predicted it would take ten years for the sea levels to rise but now, no one knew what the next minute held. The pod seemed to be floating in a pool of water already. Any sudden increase in the rise of water, it could get to the level of the pod's opening and it may just flood the entire populace. It was threatening to destroy the whole world but there was a plan C that was all over the news. The US government had stated that this would be the last hurdle the entire world would fight together as humans.

While the PRRS and other Climate-related NGOs were working tirelessly on the mission to make humans interplanetary, an eccentric billionaire, Dr.Rex had been working on an undercover mission to relocate to Mars. He had been on this mission for the last ten years and they were building large space shuttles. When he was interviewed on the news, he stated that it had always been a lifelong dream for him to explore the beauties of other planets.

"As a child, while other kids were into football, video games, and stuff, I would lock myself indoors and study science and astronomy books for hours without getting bored. I voraciously read many books on sci-fi that fed my appetite for becoming a space scientist. I've studied enough and gained degrees, now is the time for me to practice all I've learned. I've been working on my trip to Mars for almost ten years now, but I kept it undercover. Now that the world needs to be salvaged, it's high time we partnered together in relocating to other planets. It would be really hard for us to leave our beautiful planet, but the human spirit needs to survive. We are not going to give up." Dr. Rex said on the news.

The US government and other world visionaries began to partner with Dr. Rex and his team in bringing the relocation to reality. Various sectors were beginning to improvise in how their products could survive on Mars. Mr. Stanford had taught us that Mars was the most habitable planet after Earth. Now that the PRRS had collaborated with Dr. Rex, things began to move really swiftly, and the relocation scheme was materializing pretty fast.

DACKS and Brenda had begun to hold subsequent meetings and campaigns in educating the people about the need for relocation to save humanity. The turnout for the rally had been massive and we had so many teens on board. Different people asked questions about what the future held. Some stated that they were afraid of the thought of relocating, while others were excited about the whole thought of living on Mars. The campaigns and rallies were held every Friday at the park and when we realized that the crowd was mixed, Suzy suggested that we divided ourselves into groups of people that feared being interplanetary beings and another group of those who were pretty excited. When we took the tally, we surprisingly seemed to have more people in the excited category. Suzy then volunteered to talk to the ones who were scared, while Brenda and Dannie spoke with the other category.

We had just finished a rally and Brenda had decided to give us a treat in the park's restaurant.

"So, Brenda, would you like to share with us how you were able to start up this initiative at this young age? Plus, here's a quick confession, you've always been my celebrity crush ever since the day I heard you speak in the campaigns of the young farmers association, during the food crisis." Dannie said and grinned from ear to ear, his mouth full of cookies.

Brenda's cheeks were flushed and dimpled with joy before she replied. "Well, thanks for the compliment, Dannie. I've always had a thing for climate, environmental, and agricultural stuff right from when I was a girl. And so just like you guys, I volunteered with NGOs that were in line with my interests and within a few months I was a social volunteer, then I started my NGO comprising of young farmers. It's been a smooth ride all the way. When the hurdle of the food crisis came up, I was elated to help farmers work together and unite to make food available to all. The government and STF have been of great support."

We went on conversing with Brenda and she was more than eager to answer our questions. Brenda also stated that working with the PRRS has been fulfilling because she as well as DACKS was contributing and playing her part to secure the safety and hope for humanity.

Everyone had dispersed except for Andrew and me. We were in each other's embrace when I noticed a young girl was heading our direction. I figured that she might be one of the students in the rally who was still hanging around. The young girl had her hair packed into a bun with yellow ribbons and her yellow dress danced to the tune of the wind when she ran in our direction. She looked like a sunflower in her yellow outfit. By the time my eyes locked with those hazel eyes, I didn't need to be told who she was.

"Hi, Katy." She said tugging at my jeans like she used to do when she was much younger. I swept her off her feet and embraced her, twirling around until we both were dizzy. I wiped a tear from my eyes and smiled at her. Her eyes filled my entire being with warmth again.

"Good to see you again Tina. You've grown so big and beautiful in recent years." I exclaimed while she went over to give Andrew a warm hug.

"Thanks, Katy. I watched your video online about the peace rally and stuff and I told Dad I wanted to come to see you since he was coming to see Grandma and Grandpa Bryan. We arrived a few minutes after the rally ended but I'm so glad I met you. Dad's car is parked over there, we could go see him." I hurried off with Tina to see Mr. Joe

Bryan and he was delighted to see me and Andrew. He now had few streaks of grey on his hair. We talked about the relocation scheme and he also stated that he was excited about the whole idea too.

"The last time I flew a drone to fish, I realized that the water level increased a lot and it's an emergency. It wouldn't take long for the waters to swallow the pod and engulf everything in it. So, I'm super glad at what the PRRS is doing and I am glad you guys are helping. I've seen your video online. By the way, I heard they'd be visiting Mars tomorrow? "

"Yes, Mr. Bryan. Dr. Rex, his team, and other PRRS officials would be making their first trip to Mars to see what it looks like and how they can improve it for further habitation. Their take-off point is in Florida where the space shuttles are. The pod would open like a flower and they'd head right into space. They'd be there for a while. It's so good to see you again, Mr. Bryan. I guess you are heading over to your parents, right?"

"Yes, we are Katy."

"Alright. My regards to Mr. and Mrs. Bryan. Tell Mrs. Bryan I'd stop by later to catch up with her over a freshly baked pie. I've missed her pies."

"Okay. I'd tell her you said so. We got to go now. I'm glad Tina could see you." Mr. Bryan said while Tina hugged me tightly. I could still feel Tina's warmth all over me. When I got home that night, the memories of Tina and her yellow outfit ushered me into a peaceful sleep.

The first trip to Mars was successful and it was declared on the news that preparations were ongoing. Dr. Rex and his team had described their experience on Mars. He also stated that the travel time to Mars wasn't as tedious as it used to be in the earlier times. Technology and space shuttles had made the trips easier. One of the geologists that traveled with the team said that the soil on Mars was good for human survival and that plans were ongoing to make machines that could extract water from the soil on Mars. While listening to the news, I grabbed my phone to read more about Mars online.

I discovered that Mars had a layer of atmosphere thinner than that of Earth. It also contained trace levels of oxygen, carbon monoxide, water vapor, hydrogen, and other noble gases. Plants such as sweet potatoes, garlic, kale, lettuce, carrots, dandelions, and basil were robust crops that grew on the Martian soil. Dad and mom listened closely while I read out the online information about Mars aloud. In the concluding interview of Dr.Rex and team, he stated that there was enough sunlight to power solar panels on Mars and that would serve as a source of electricity and lighting. He added that space elevators would be used to land people and material on Mars.

"I really do feel like relocating to Mars this minute. It sounds like a whole lot of adventure you know. All we need is a cup of coffee and a hug, wherever we live. What do you say to that baby?" Dad said with laughter written all over his face.

"Yeah, honey. I'm excited already." Mom said before hugging me and Dad.

That day was no different, nothing exceptional happened. The sun was smiling brightly. I could hear the birds tweeting their usual morning songs. Even the wind blew by softly. It was a normal morning but the birds in my heart were tweeting a somber song. While I was busy working on my computer and writing a speech for the next rally, while dad was busy working in his shed. My mobile phone started ringing. I realized it was an unknown number and I ignored it. But the caller wouldn't relent and when I couldn't take it anymore, I picked the call while a gentle, male voice responded over the phone.

"Hello. Am I talking to Miss Katy?"

"Yes. Who am I speaking with please?"

"I am officer Peter Matthews. There has been an accident involving two cars. We found a phone in one of the cars. I figured your number was the last dialed. I..."

"Where is my mom right now? What happened? How bad is it? When did it happen? Oh my God!!" I attacked the police officer with questions, not even sparing him a minute to answer.

"Calm down ma'am. Just calm down. The body has been transferred to New Havens Hospital."

The moment I heard the word 'body', I knew I was never going to see mom again. Mom was never going to witness Mars. She wasn't going to know what it felt like to experience the adventures of another planet. Mom was never going to watch the news or laugh or plant kisses on my forehead anymore. Mom had gone on a trip with death, and she was never coming back.

I wasn't the same person anymore. The sun felt coy the day mom was lowered into the ground. Dad, neighbors, friends, classmates, family all paid their respect. I stood glued to the ground, my eyes locking with the spot where mom had just been laid. All I wanted was to wash the feeling of grief that I had on. I wanted to remain till I was submerged underwater and buried six feet just like mom. It was Andrew that could proffer comfort at that time, he's been in my shoes before. We both had a common loss, our moms were staring right back at us from beneath the ground.

Few months after mom's demise, the PRRS and the entire US government were ready to launch their first relocation mission to Mars. They had stated that they would begin the relocation of the first batch of people who were ready to relocate with families. Over time, they had been making numerous trips to Mars, installing technological equipment and all other infrastructures to make the place comfy and habitable. Among the first batch of the mission team, DACKS, Brenda and her team, STF, and all other climate-related NGOs were given the honor to be the first set of people to inhabit Mars.

When Cassy and Suzy shared the news with me, I gave off a weak smile. They had come for a girl's night out to give me company. Dad had buried himself with work just to take his mind off mom's demise and he hardly said a word. His face did all the talking instead. Kula had also been whimpering. It seemed like the poor dog knew one person was missing in the house. When I wasn't showing up for meetings and rallies, Cassy and Suzy had both decided to spend at least two nights a week at my place just to cheer me up and stay close. They were the best four-eyed girlfriends I could ever ask for.

"Wow. We are being considered as one of the first to enjoy the comfort of Mars before others join us. That's cool girls." Cassy exclaimed and jumped all over the room, her glasses almost fell off her face. Suzy also had a huge smile on.

"I ain't going guys," I replied, and Cassy and Suzy were alarmed.

"Just kidding babes. I just wanted to scare you guys. Sure, I'm in. It's a reality. It was part of mom's numerous wishes. She wanted to go to Mars and feel the adventures of being an interplanetary human. She wanted to get her hands in the Martian soil and taste the crops that grew there. So, I'm gonna fulfill mom's wish. I feel like she is in me. I am her. I'm going to survive, no matter the cost." Cassy and Suzy already wrapped me up in a warm embrace even before I finished speaking. All I could do was smile amidst the pool of tears welling up in my eyes.

After Cassy and Suzy left, I went into a deep train of thoughts that made me think. We survived so far with human ingenuity and creativity. Is it the new beginning for humans? Or is it the beginning of the end?

The human body might be mortal but not the spirit!

Acknowledgments

I would like to thank every reader who finished this book. It was a pleasure sharing this story with you guys. I would like to thank Laurette, Soumya, and David who helped me edit this book. Irrespective of multiple efforts from different people there might be a few grammatical mistakes that may have been left out unintentionally. I hope you guys enjoyed the story, as much as I did writing it.

2020 was a challenging year for us all. With human ingenuity, scientists came up with a vaccine in a record time. When humans are pushed to a corner, the human spirit can make the impossible possible. Special thanks to all the brave men and women, who are willing to sacrifice their lives for a greater cause. We are interdependent species, everything we possess today is made by someone else, including the paper in your hand. Let's be thankful for life.

What are you thankful for?

159